Victorian Bride

Moment in Time, Volume 2

Lexy Timms

Published by Dark Shadow Publishing, 2016.

This is a work of fiction. Similarities to real people, places, or events are entirely coincidental.

VICTORIAN BRIDE

First edition. November 6, 2016.

Copyright © 2016 Lexy Timms.

Written by Lexy Timms.

Also by Lexy Timms

Alpha Bad Boy Motorcycle Club Triology
Alpha Biker

Conquering Warrior Series
Ruthless

Diamond in the Rough Anthology
Billionaire Rock
Billionaire Rock - part 2

Dominating PA Series
Her Personal Assistant - Part 1
Her Personal Assistant - Part 2
Her Personal Assistant - Part 3
Her Personal Assistant Box Set

Firehouse Romance Series
Caught in Flames
Burning With Desire
Craving the Heat
Firehouse Romance Complete Collection

Fortune Riders MC Series
Billionaire Biker
Billionaire Ransom
Billionaire Misery

Hades' Spawn Motorcycle Club
One You Can't Forget
One That Got Away

One That Came Back
One You Never Leave
Hades' Spawn MC Complete Series

Heart of the Battle Series
Celtic Viking
Celtic Rune
Celtic Mann
Heart of the Battle Series Box Set

Justice Series
Seeking Justice
Finding Justice
Chasing Justice
Pursuing Justice
Justice - Complete Series

Love You Series
Love Life: Billionaire Dance School Hot Romance
Need Love

Managing the Bosses Series
The Boss
The Boss Too
Who's the Boss Now
Love the Boss
I Do the Boss
Wife to the Boss
Employed by the Boss
Brother to the Boss
Senior Advisor to the Boss
Forever the Boss
Gift for the Boss - Novella 3.5

Moment in Time
Highlander's Bride
Victorian Bride
Modern Day Bride

R&S Rich and Single Series
Alex Reid
Parker

Saving Forever
Saving Forever - Part 1
Saving Forever - Part 2
Saving Forever - Part 3
Saving Forever - Part 4
Saving Forever - Part 5
Saving Forever - Part 6
Saving Forever Part 7
Saving Forever - Part 8

Southern Romance Series
Little Love Affair
Siege of the Heart
Freedom Forever
Soldier's Fortune

Tattooist Series
Confession of a Tattooist
Surrender of a Tattooist
Heart of a Tattooist

Tennessee Romance
Whisky Lullaby
Whisky Melody
Whisky Harmony

The Debt
The Debt: Part 1 - Damn Horse
The Debt: Complete Collection

The University of Gatica Series
The Recruiting Trip
Faster
Higher
Stronger
Dominate
No Rush

Undercover Series
Perfect For Me
Perfect For You
Perfect For Us

Unknown Identity Series
Unknown
Unexposed
Unpublished

Standalone
Wash
Loving Charity
Summer Lovin'
Christmas Magic: A Romance Anthology
Love & College
Billionaire Heart
First Love
Frisky and Fun Romance Box Collection
Managing the Bosses Box Set #1-3

Victorian Bride
Moment in Time: Book #2
By Lexy Timms
Copyright 2016 Lexy Timms

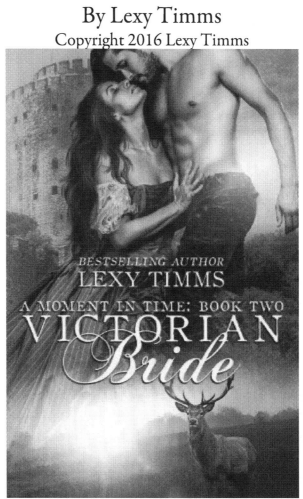

All rights reserved. No part of this publication may be reproduced, stored in or introduced into a retrieval system, or transmitted, in any form, or by any means (electronic, mechanical, photocopying, recording, or otherwise) without the prior written permission of both the copyright owner and the above publisher of this book.

This is a work of fiction. Names, characters, places, brands, media, and incidents are either the product of the author's imagination or are used fictitiously. Any resemblance to an actual person, living or dead, events, or locales is entirely coincidental. The author acknowledges the trademarked status and trademark owners of various products referenced in this work of fiction, which have been used without permission. The publication/use of these trademarks is not authorized, associated with, or sponsored by the trademark owners.

All rights reserved.
Copyright 2016 by Lexy Timms
Cover: Book Cover by Design

A Moment in Time Series

Highlander's Bride
Book 1
Victorian Bride
Book 2
Modern Day Bride
Book 3
A Royal Bride
Book 4
Forever the Bride
Book 5

Find Lexy Timms:

Lexy Timms Newsletter:
http://eepurl.com/9i0vD
Lexy Timms Facebook Page:
https://www.facebook.com/SavingForever

Lexy Timms Website:
http://lexytimms.wix.com/savingforever

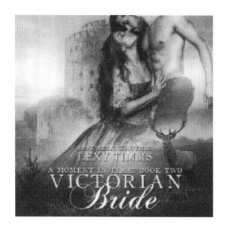

Description

Remember enough of the past... You may be able to control the future.

She shouldn't be here... She doesn't even know how she got here.

There is always the dream. Mya can't recall all the details, but it wakes her up at night in a cold sweat with fear sending her heart racing.

Mya wakes in a bed she doesn't recognize, in a house she doesn't know. A woman tells her that they found her in their fields and have been taking care of her. As she gazes out the window, she sees a stag. A brilliant beast, white fur and strong, large antlers.

She also finds a scar on her shoulder that she doesn't remember getting.

A grown woman with no memory, no family, no money.

Kayden McGregor, a Scotsman who seems more a Highlander, owns an estate near where she is staying. When they meet, there is a fire between the two of them—and it's impossible to tell if it's fury or passion.

She resents him. He can't bear to look at her. Or stop himself from staring when Mya pretends not to notice. Trapped, and yet somehow destined to be together.

"You were made to be with me, as I was made to love you. No moment in time can take that away from us."

Prologue

Mya ran.

Behind her ribs she could feel the beat of her heart, steady and strong. Her legs pumped, carrying her, swift and easy. The sensation of air flowing over her skin and filling her lungs made her light. Beside her, she could feel another presence, matching her stride. They ran for the joy of it, just because they could, and it filled her up, overflowing in her chest. She bounded over a rock, and he jumped at her side.

Her footing faltered.

Mya stumbled. Something in her body shifted, and her feet became clumsy. Her legs would not obey her commands. The world looked strange around her, seen through eyes that were unfamiliar. She managed to catch herself before falling. It took a moment but she was able to start moving again.

Overhead, thunder crashed, unrolling itself across the clouds with a deep, displeased rumble. Lightning forked down, burning the skeletons of trees across the backs of her eyelids in silhouette. Her companion was gone. He hadn't stumbled. He'd run ahead, and in the darkness she had lost him. She ran on alone, because she had to. Fear drove her forward. There was no time, and she could not remember what she searched for.

Rain fell, sharp as needles. It pricked against her skin and chilled her through. To her left, she could hear the sound of surf falling against shoreline, violent and ragged as the wind that drove it. She shivered, and pushed her stumbling legs forward. Wet hair tumbled into her eyes and clung to her cheeks, obstructing her vision. She reached up to push it back.

Thunder boomed, and the earth split. The ground went out from under her feet.

Mya fell.

There was nothing for her grasping hands to catch. Only emptiness beneath her, and pain. Stabbing. Tearing. Pain that ripped through her chest and left her gasping in shock, struggling to breathe. Worse than anything she'd ever experienced. Enough pain to tear a heart. It burned along her veins.

A scream forced its way up from the depths of her, but no sound escaped, all the air gone from her lungs, her throat tight.

The pain dragged her up toward the light.

She woke.

Chapter 1

M‌ya came slowly up from the depths of unconsciousness.

Her first awareness was of quiet. Her ears rang with echoes of thunder she didn't remember. She let her senses roam outward, trying to determine her position without opening her eyes. There was something soft beneath her. A bed, maybe. The warmth of a heavy blanket covered her.

She took a deep breath, smelling clean linen, and the faint scent of cooking drifting into the room from somewhere else. For a moment, she simply lay still, basking in the peace of it. That didn't last long.

There was something whispering at the back of her mind. A worry that she couldn't quite put a name to. When she tried to reach for it, the warning slid further from her reach. The last vestiges of a dream, maybe, lingering at the edges of her thoughts before the daylight melted it away completely. It was not enough to aid her, in any case. Mya shook off the concern and opened her eyes to discover her surroundings.

The room wasn't what she had expected. Though what, exactly, she had thought it would be, she couldn't have explained. Smaller, maybe. Some part of her had thought it would be... Not this. She couldn't pinpoint more than that.

It was spacious, papered in cream and sky blue, and paneled in wood that gleamed the color of honey in the light spilling through the windows. A chest of drawers in the same wood sat against one wall, topped with a tall oval mirror. Next to the bed was a cabinet with a washbasin and pitcher sitting atop it. A pair of pastel pink chairs faced each other in front of the high arched windows, a little table between them. Through the glass, Mya could see a sloping yard set here and there with trees, and behind it purple hills rising up toward a blue and cloudless sky.

Mya didn't recognize it.

How had she arrived there? She tried to think back, to trace memories that might have led to the bed she was lying in, but there was nothing. Just blankness. Emptiness. It was as though all the time before that moment when she first returned to awareness had never existed at all.

She knew her name, and the names of the things around her, but she could not remember where she'd learned them. Or when. It was a disconcerting realization.

"Oh. My."

The voice from the door startled her, and Mya levered herself upright on one elbow, turning to see who spoke. Or, at least, she attempted to. The motion sent a jolt of pain through her shoulder that had her collapsing back to the mattress with a gasp, panting for breath.

"You ought not to move, dear," the voice that had spoken before said, low and worried, just as its owner bustled into Mya's view.

She was tall, clad in a gown patterned with sprays of pale green leaves and belted at her waist. As she reached Mya, she laid a hand on her forehead, tutting at whatever she discovered there.

"You are meant to be resting," she said as she turned to the basin sitting beside the bed and wrung water from the cloth sitting in it. "Young Lord McGregor found you in our back field, badly injured. It was quite uncertain for a time whether you would wake at all. Lottie was quite firm in her belief that you would, but even Doctor MacAslan had his doubts in the first days of your stay with us."

She was, Mya thought, rather pretty, perhaps a few years older than Mya herself, her pale hair touched with red. She laid the damp cloth over Mya's forehead, and stroked her hair gently back from her face so it would not catch.

"I need to take a look at your shoulder," she went on while Mya was still trying to process everything she had just learned. "If it will not trouble you for me to do so?"

Mutely, still not sure what to say, Mya shook her head. The woman folded back the blanket that covered her, revealing the nightgown she wore, which was partially unbuttoned to allow access to her shoulder.

"It has not begun to bleed again, I think," the woman said, when she had tugged the nightgown gently out of the way to check the bandage. "The doctor did wish me to tell you, though, if you woke while he was gone, to take care in using that arm. You have healing yet to do."

It occurred to her, abruptly, that the woman had spoken of days.

"How long have I been here?" she asked, the voice leaving her throat rough with disuse. She timidly tried to clear it.

"Three days," the woman answered. "We thought it best to keep you with us while you were unconscious, as we had no way of knowing who your family might be, and you were comfortably set up here."

Mya wasn't sure how to say that she had no way of knowing who her family might be either. The woman was looking at her expectantly, as though she awaited some sort of answer to the unspoken question.

"I..." Mya took a breath and let it out again. "I don't remember."

"You do not remember what, dear?"

"The accident. How I was injured. Or... my family." She bit her lip, glancing away from the serious blue eyes studying her. "I don't remember anything before waking up here."

There was a long moment of silence.

Mya was sure if she looked up she'd find the woman staring back at her. She had already watched over her for three days. They surely wouldn't be interested in keeping her around much longer when she couldn't pay rent or offer any useful skills. She wondered if there was protocol for that sort of thing. Would the lady, the doctor and whoever else, tell her where she might find lodging if she couldn't afford it? When she couldn't remember who she was or where she was from? Did she even have something to pay for her care?

"Nothing?" the woman asked finally.

Mya shook her head. "Not a thing," she admitted. "I tried. Everything is just blank. This empty space where memories should be."

"We will speak with the doctor about it." The woman reached out and turned the cloth on Mya's forehead over so the cool side rested against her skin. "And you need not worry about being thrown out, if you fear that. Lottie and I would not put someone out onto the streets with nowhere to go and no memory of her kin."

"You've given enough of your time already," Mya said. "I shouldn't take up more of it."

"Nonsense." When she finally looked up, the woman smiled at her. "We wouldn't hear of you wandering about Inverness with no memory and no money to your name. All that, and the clothes you were wearing when you were found are rightly ruined. You've nothing suitable to wear in public, so you shall just have to stay."

Mya opened her mouth to speak, and shut it again when she was stopped before she could start.

"You will not even think of arguing. I've made up my mind, and there's nothing to be done for it. You will remain here with us until we can find someone who knows where you are meant to be, or else until you have the means to strike out on your own. I will not hear otherwise."

The words were sharp, but Mya could see the smile hiding beneath them, and secretly she was grateful. If she wasn't allowed to argue, she would simply have to stay, and the knowledge that she wouldn't be turned out into the streets of an unfamiliar city was more of a relief than she cared to admit.

"Thank you," she said. "You are so kind—I don' t know how to repay you for such generosity."

Her benefactor lifted one shoulder in a shrug and let it fall again. "You need not, dear. We do what we believe is right, and what is right is aiding a stranger in need."

She stood, then, and picked up a cup from the cabinet top, which she offered to Mya, helping her sit up against the pillows so she could hold the cup in her good hand and drink.

"Now then," the woman said when she had finished drinking and given the cup back. "I imagine that you must be hungry."

Mya hadn't been; she'd hardly had time to think of her stomach with everything else that was going on, but once the words were spoken she realized that she was, in fact, quite hungry. If she had been in bed unconscious for three days, it had been at least that long since she had eaten, and the hollow ache in her stomach made itself painfully apparent.

"Yes," she said, voice a little smoother after the glass of water. "I could stand to eat."

"Lottie should just be sitting down to breakfast. We shall go and join her."

She slipped an arm under Mya's good shoulder again, helping her sit up. Mya swung her feet around to settle against the sleek wood of the floor, and slowly stood upright, using her good arm to catch herself against the mattress when her knees nearly buckled beneath her.

"Slowly," the woman said. "Doctor MacAslan said that you would need to go carefully when you first got out of bed. You've been unconscious for quite some time."

Slowly. Mya stood a little more carefully, the supporting arm still strong around her waist, and found herself steady on her feet.

"I'm not wearing anything suitable for breakfast," she said, looking between her nightgown and the clothing the woman in front of her wore, but her hostess simply shook her head.

"That is hardly of import when you have been so ill. We will find some clothing for you this afternoon, if need be, though in truth I think you will have to rest again. I believe you are close enough to Lottie's size to borrow a few of her things, if necessary, while we have something made up for you."

"I do not have money to—"

The woman waved away the rest of the words. "Lottie and I are blessed with more than enough to get by. If you wish to repay us when you have found work, or your family, we will discuss it, but until then do not even think of the money. As I said, we do what is right."

She slipped her arm through Mya's then, guiding her out into the hall. Mya blinked back the prickling sting of grateful tears, turning toward the windows that lined the passageway.

They looked out on the same neatly trimmed green lawn as the window in the bedroom where she'd woken. At the top of its slope, a stag stood calmly grazing, his hide ivory white in the sun. As though he sensed her eyes on him, he slowly lifted his head, turning his gaze to her. Mya's footsteps faltered, nearly a stumble before the woman beside her caught her weight.

"Are you well?" she asked, worry obvious in her voice.

Mya dragged her gaze from the stag to find her hostess regarding her with concern.

"Fine. Thank you," she answered.

When she turned to look back out the windows, the stag was gone.

Chapter 2

Her guide led Mya not to a room in the house, but out through a set of doors to a veranda on the side of the house opposite the lawn. Its paving stones were warm beneath her bare feet. A breeze, just cool enough to be pleasant, brushed against her cheek, smelling of green things and wildflowers and breakfast. Mya's stomach growled. Beyond the porch, the lawn gave way to a wooded slope rolling down into patchwork fields bordered with hedges. White dots of sheep moved peacefully over them.

Back on the porch, at a cast-iron table much burdened with food, a dark-haired young woman was sitting with a book in one hand, sipping a cup of tea. She rose at the sound of them stepping outside and turned, a smile lighting her face when she saw Mya and her hostess standing there.

She was, Mya couldn't help but notice, almost astonishingly beautiful, with the kind of looks that would have men falling over themselves to court her.

"Eleanora," she said warmly, setting the book she had been reading down and crossing the veranda to take the other woman's free hand in hers. "Good morning." Her gaze moved to Mya. "And to you as well. It is so lovely to see you awake. Please, do come sit and eat with me."

Mya found herself being guided over to the table before she even had time to answer, and placed gently down in a well-cushioned seat.

"Help yourself to anything you like," Eleanora said.

The breakfast spread was, Mya thought, a little overwhelming. There was fruit laid out on china plates, and yogurt in little bowls. Eggs. Buttered toast. Sausages and mushrooms. She hesitated a moment before reaching a little uncertainly for the kettle to pour herself a cup of tea.

"No need to be shy," the dark-haired woman, whom Mya assumed to be the Lottie earlier referenced by Eleanora, said. "Everything here is for sharing."

"Thank you," Mya said, wishing she had some more adequate way of expressing gratitude. "Very much." She poured herself the cup, and after some consideration served herself fruit and toast with some of the mushrooms.

"You ought to try the smoked fish as well," Eleanora suggested, indicating one of the plates. "It is quite good."

Mya added a little of the dish to her collection of food. If she hadn't eaten in a few days, would her stomach handle it? She decided to take her time, even though everything smelled beyond delicious.

"It occurs to me," Lottie said, "that we have not yet introduced ourselves. I'm terribly sorry for our dreadful lapse in manners." She smiled across the table at Mya. "I'm Ottilie, though most everyone calls me Lottie, and this is Eleanora."

She knew her name, like she knew she needed to breath to keep her heart beating. It seemed weird to know that, and only that. "Mya." She frowned. "I'm not sure why I know my name, as at the moment, I don't seem to know anything else." She smiled apologetically. "I cannot tell you how grateful I am for your aid."

Lottie shook her head. "It is hardly trouble. I've more money than I know what to do with." She said the words as though they were some sort of delightful secret. "In truth, I would rather it go toward helping those in need than to frivolities in the shops. I do not need any more gowns."

Eleanora laughed. "You would require a second—or third—closet, I think, if you acquired many more."

There was, Mya noted, no ring on either of their fingers, and she wondered how long they had been sharing the home they were letting her stay in, and where the money that Lottie seemed to think so little of had come from. She didn't ask. Though she could not remember any etiquette lessons she might have learned any more than she could recall the rest of her past, she had enough common sense not to stick her nose into someone else's financial business without an invitation.

"I have a dreadful addiction to nice clothing," Lottie said between dainty bites of egg and fish. "It is undoubtedly a sin of some sort or another."

"Avarice," Eleanora suggested.

Lottie turned to look at her, mock-displeasure on her face. "Are you accusing me of such, then?"

"I would not dream of accusing you, dearest."

Mya smiled down at her plate. They sounded for all the world like an old married couple, though how she knew what an old married couple sounded like, she wasn't entirely sure. The knowledge without source was rather frustrating. For an instant, she thought she could remember sharing such teasing, laughter and... But the memory was gone again almost before it had appeared, and Mya could not recall what she had been thinking of. She sighed and turned her attention back to Lottie and Eleanora, who were engaged in a spirited debate over just how many gowns qualified as too many.

"Mya will be on my side," Lottie said finally.

"I think," Eleanora chuckled, "That you are rather mistaken in that."

Lottie gave her a narrow-eyed look, and turned a sweet smile on Mya. "Tell me, dear, what is your opinion on the matter? How many gowns are too many?"

"I don't think I really have the experience to comment," Mya said, taking a sip of tea.

That earned light laughter from both her hosts.

"Clever," Eleanora said, with a conspiratorial smile for Mya. "A very eloquent answer."

Mya hid a smile in her teacup.

"Doctor MacAslan will be here later in the afternoon to check on you," Lottie said, the laughter faded from her voice and her dark eyes fixed on Mya. "I'm certain he will be quite pleased to see you awake. In the meantime, I thought perhaps we might take a stroll through the gardens, if you would be interested in such a thing? Or if you are tired you are welcome to return to your room, or rest on the couch in my studio, if you wish for someone to talk to."

It was a lovely summer day, the first fluffy clouds just beginning to drift across the blue vault of the sky. "A walk in the gardens sounds wonderful, actually."

Lottie's smile lit up her face. "A garden walk it is, then. Will you be joining us, Eleanora?"

"Unfortunately, I have work to attend to, but perhaps another morning." Eleanora set aside her napkin and rose from her chair, nodding a farewell to each of them in turn before she disappeared back into the house.

"She's a much harder worker than I am," Lottie said, in the tone of one confiding a secret. "Though of course we hardly need the money."

"Does she enjoy it, then?" Mya asked, setting her fork and knife across her plate the way she had seen Eleanora do. Interesting that the two women's focus was money. Why was that?

"Oh. Quite. Writing has always been rather a passion of hers." Lottie too laid her utensils on her plate, though more carelessly than Mya had, and stood. "Shall we?"

Mya got carefully to her feet, leaning a little on the table with her good hand before she straightened up. "Lead on, then."

As Eleanora had, Lottie slipped her arm through Mya's, and they walked together around the corner of the veranda and down a set of wide stone steps into the backyard.

"There is a greenhouse on the other side of the building," Lottie said. "If you would like to visit that later."

She paused, glancing down at Mya's bare feet, clearly visible beneath the hem of her nightgown.

"I forgot to ask you if you would like shoes," she said. "I'm not certain I have any of a size that would fit you, but we could take a look, if you wish to wear them. There may at least be house slippers."

Mya shook her head. She felt more comfortable barefoot. The grass was soft and cool under her feet in the shade of the tree that overhung the porch, and she wanted to feel the earth beneath her. Not the uncomfortable soles of someone else's shoes.

Lottie smiled. "I'm not wearing any either," she admitted. "I rather hate the things, if I am honest. And there is hardly anyone to care here at the manor. The servants undoubtedly gossip about it, but it will be just one more eccentricity Lottie Alan has picked up. The general populace love to pretend as though they are scandalized by such things."

"Do you think they aren't?" Mya asked.

They were moving out of the shade and into the sunlight, and she turned her face up toward it, basking in the warmth on her skin.

"I think they wish they had the courage to do it themselves. Which sounds arrogant, I suppose, but it is not as though it is an act of valor. Especially here, where I am allowed to do as I please, for the most part, so long as word of the worst offenses against society does not get out."

There was a quirk to her mouth that said the explanation was at least a little exaggerated, though Mya wondered how much of it was a joke, and how much of the joke was truth.

"It's your own property."

"Yes," Lottie agreed. "And since James died and left it to me, I've found that I do not care so much for what others think."

James. Mya didn't ask who he was, despite the way the question was burning on the tip of her tongue.

"I can see you are dying to ask." Lottie laughed. "James is my late husband. We were married quite young, and he didn't live to see our second wedding anniversary." Her expression softened to something almost sad. "He was a good man, despite being English, and left me more than was required of him. Most are not so lucky as I was. He was so sweet. So handsome. So... James."

"Do you think you will remarry?" Mya asked. She wasn't sure if the question was impolite. It just seemed that Lottie was too young to be alone. She had Eleanora, but it wasn't the same.

Lottie gave the question only a moment's thought before she shook her head, the curls of her chignon dancing against the nape of her neck. "No," she said. "It is hardly in a man's favor to wed me now, when I have the right to keep them from meddling with James' property. If they cannot steal my wealth off me, they have much less reason to woo me." She smiled. "And, in truth, I am happy as I am. Eleanora and I get along well here. We are both free to pursue our interests as we please, spend our money as we please, and generally live as we choose. It is not a bad life to live."

"I didn't realize it was so..." Mya wasn't sure what the word she sought was.

"Restrictive?" Lottie suggested as they stepped onto a path of smooth paving stones that wound through a carpet of bright bluebells.

The delicate scent of the flowers filled the air around them, and Mya, breathing it in, felt as though she had walked in such a place before. But she could not recall where, or when. Ahead, a latticework gazebo grew pink climbing roses. Lottie led her to a bench beneath one of the arches and they sat there together, breathing in the heady perfume of the blossoms, deeper and richer than the barely there scent of the bluebells.

"I suppose that is one way to describe it," Lottie said. "Though it does depend somewhat on the man. James was never fond of controlling me. Perhaps he knew how useless it was to try." There, again, was the flash of her smile, bright and amused.

"Did you love him?" Mya asked. She wanted that. The love that could move mountains. That could make time stand still. It was silly to think of that right now. She didn't know who she was or if she already had someone. She might even have a loving husband at a home, waiting anxiously for her. She might have... She sighed. She hoped Lottie had that kind of love with James.

Lottie was silent for longer than Mya would have expected, and she almost regretted asking the question.

"I'm sorry," she started to say. "I—"

"No," Lottie interrupted. "Do not concern yourself. It's not a bad question, only one that is not simple to answer." She looked down at her hands, folded together in her lap. "James and I didn't know each other well before our marriage. We courted, of course, but it was more a business match than a love match. We did, in time, grow fond of each other, and I suppose what we had could be called love, but it was not the romantic ardor I think you meant when you asked."

"I think I was in love," Mya said.

It was a thought that had been building throughout their conversation, making itself impossible to ignore. She did not know quite where it came from, but it was there all the same. Blurting it out to a woman who was still almost a stranger didn't entirely seem like the solution, but Mya couldn't help feeling that the woman sitting beside her would understand.

Lottie turned to look at her, brows raised in question. "What makes you say so?"

It was Mya's turn to be silent, wrestling with her own inability to describe the certainty settled somewhere deep in her chest. Like the phantom ache of another heart beating next to her own. There was meant to be someone beside her.

"I feel it," she said finally. "It's not a satisfactory explanation, I know, but I don't know how to describe it any further."

"You need not." Lottie reached up and plucked a rose from the vine winding its way along the wrought-iron leg of the gazebo. She turned the bloom over in her hands, stroking the soft petals with the tips of her fingers. "Some things simply are. We know them, and we cannot describe them, because the truth of them is deeper than the flimsy construct of words. Perhaps Eleanora could make a better attempt of it, but some things, I think, are not meant to be spoken. It is why I use a paintbrush and not a pen."

Mya thought of the white stag, turning his head to meet her gaze with his great, dark eyes, and the way her chest had filled with something bright and nameless at the sight of it. The stag. She couldn't remember things, but she remembered the handsome beast?

Without memory through which to view the world, too many of the things rattling around inside her had no words to describe them. No context in which to place them.

Perhaps, she thought, Lottie was right. Maybe some things were better left unsaid. Maybe even with her memories, she wouldn't know how to put words to the feelings that welled up in her. She breathed in the peace of the garden, and side by side they sat in companionable silence, neither of them saying anything at all.

Chapter 3

"We can come sit with you when the doctor arrives," Lottie offered as they made their way back up the path to the house. "If you would prefer it. He's a very kind man, and you have nothing to fear from him, but I know how intimidating such encounters can be. You've been... well, out each time he's come."

"I would like that, honestly," Mya admitted.

"One or both of us shall rescue you, then," Lottie promised. "If nothing else, medical checkups are not terribly exciting, and we would not wish you to suffer. Eleanora would be quite put out with me for failing as a hostess." She didn't quite manage to keep a straight face as she said it, a smile playing at the corners of her mouth and her dark eyes glittering with suppressed laughter.

Mya, despite the slight nervousness incited by the mention of the doctor's visit and concern for what it might reveal about her health, found herself giggling. "I believe agreeing to put me up indefinitely for free makes you both incomparable hostesses, purely by virtue of that action."

"Well, for heaven's sake, do not tell Ella that. If she thinks she has to impress you, we'll get to go to more parties."

"Are you telling me that you're using me as an excuse to go shock high society?"

Lottie gave her a wide-eyed innocent look that Mya didn't believe for a minute. "I cannot believe you would accuse me of such a thing."

Mya shook her head, laughing, and then winced at the pain in her shoulder. "I've known you for all of four hours, and I already know better than to trust that expression on your face."

Laughing, Lottie led her up the steps onto the porch. "Ella always falls for it, you know."

"I don't believe Ella does fall for it," Mya retorted. "I think she just indulges you and your whims."

Lottie attempted a wounded expression that dissolved almost instantly into hard laughter. "You," she said, panting to catch her breath, "are entirely too clever for my own good. Do you not know it is rude to call your hostess out on her little self-delusions?"

"I thought we were just discussing your fondness for bending the rules of proper behavior."

The dark-haired woman threw her free hand in the air. "I give up. You have defeated me utterly," she said, chuckling once more.

A disappointingly easy venture, Mya almost said. The words hovered on the tip of her tongue, but she did not speak them. They were, after all, still nearly strangers, and she was a guest in Lottie's home. She had no wish to cross a line that would offend. Instead, she merely smiled. Lottie gave her a look that said she knew what Mya was thinking, or at least that she was thinking something of the sort, but didn't press her to speak the words aloud.

"Unfortunately, as much as I would enjoy remaining here with you and continuing this conversation, I have a letter I must write before the day is out. Do you wish to return to your room, or would you prefer to remain outside?"

"I would like to stay here, I think," Mya decided. "And enjoy the weather."

"An excellent choice." Lottie made certain Mya was steady on her feet before stepping back. "I will send the maid to fetch you when the doctor arrives, and we'll make certain you have company for the visit."

"Thank you. Again. For everything," Mya said, taking a seat on one of the padded benches that sat along the back of the porch. "I'll be here."

Lottie nodded in understanding and went inside, pausing at the door to give Mya a little wave before she hurried off.

At least, Mya thought as she turned her eyes to the landscape below the house, staying here would not be dull.

When the doctor arrived, Mya was very nearly dozing. The maid who came to collect her had to say her name twice to get her attention, and looked a little amused when Mya startled up from the seat, blinking away the lingering sleepy lassitude.

"Doctor MacAslan here to see you, ma'am," she said when Mya had turned to look at her, her startled heart still beating a little too fast in her chest.

"Thank you," Mya said, touching her shoulder gingerly. The maid turned and Mya took a step after her. "Could you show me where I'm meant to meet him, please?"

"Yes, ma'am. If you'll just follow me."

Relieved that she wouldn't be expected to find her way through the still unfamiliar house on her own, Mya followed the maid inside and down the maze of halls to the room where she had woken. Thankfully the maid's guidance probably saved her several wrong turns.

Both Lottie and Eleanora were there already, talking with a gray-haired man in a suit. His doctor's bag sat on top of the cupboard beside the bed with the washbasin. When Mya entered, all three of them turned to look at her. Eleanora, she noted, was wearing a pink rose in her hair, tucked just behind her ear.

"Miss Mya, it is, I presume?" the doctor asked. It wasn't really a question. He knew exactly who she was, considering that he had been treating her for the past three days, but she supposed he hadn't actually known her name.

"Yes... Sir." Mya tacked on the respectful address a little too late to make them believe she had actually planned to use it, but the doctor only smiled. He had the kind of face that was easy to trust, open and honest, with lines at the corners of his eyes that suggested he spent much of his time smiling. Some of the nerves that had returned at the maid's summons settled themselves.

"It is good to see you up and about." Doctor MacAslan directed her as he spoke, beckoning her forward to sit on the edge of the bed while he retrieved a stethoscope from his bag. "It was a bit touch and go for a few days."

He pressed the tube of the stethoscope to her chest and had her breathe, then repeated the procedure at her back. "Your heart seems well enough," he said, leaning in next to examine her eyes. "Are you having any unexplained aches or pains? Any physical trouble?"

"My shoulder hurts," Mya said. "But I think you are aware of that already."

The doctor smiled. "Quite aware. We will take a look at that in a moment."

True to his word, he had her lie back against the pillows and folded the nightgown back to bare her shoulder. Carefully, he loosened the bandage that covered the wound.

Looking down, Mya could see that it had almost healed. Or, at least, it looked that way to her, though to her knowledge she had no medical training. But the wound was entirely closed, only slightly red at its edges. The raised scab that marked it was not entirely pleasant to look at, but she took from Doctor MacAslan's pleased muttering that it was a good sign.

He pressed his fingertips down against the flesh around the mark, and asked her at various times if it hurt. Mya shook her head. It felt a little tender, but there was no sharp pain. When the doctor straightened up, he had a smile on his face.

"You are coming along quite well," he said, packing the tools he had used back into his bag as he spoke. "You ought to still be careful of how you use that arm—vigorous exertion could cause pain or even reopen parts of the wound—but I believe that in time you shall get the full use of the limb back. And in a fortnight or so, the pain should be gone entirely."

"Can she travel?" Lottie asked.

The doctor turned to look at her. "I cannot see why she should not. So long as she does not lift anything too heavy. But a trip into town will hardly be dangerous for her."

"Thank you, Doctor," Mya said, glancing at her caretakers and wondering what they were planning. She'd just woken, and wasn't sure how much energy she'd have, even though she did feel quite rested. It was all strange.

"Don't thank me yet, Miss Mya," he said and winked. "I'm not finished with my examination."

"Oh."

He patted her hand. "Don't be anxious, my dear. I'm here to help."

She gave him a hesitant smile.

He sat in the chair at the desk and pulled out a leather notebook. He pulled out a pen and using the ink on the desk, filled it and wrote a few notes down. "The ladies mentioned that you remember your name is Mya, yes?"

"Yes."

"Do you remember anything else?"

Mya squinted, trying to press the recesses of her mind for some kind of knowledge, but she couldn't pull a memory or fragment from it. "Mya... Boyle," she said suddenly. "Boyle. Mya Boyle."

"Hmmm..." The doctor wrote something down in his notes. "You know your name?"

She nodded.

"Family?"

"I... I don't think so."

Lottie cleared her throat. "She mentioned she felt that she'd been in love before."

"Married?" the doctor asked.

Mya shook her head slowly. "I don't know... I don't think so."

"Father? Mother? Siblings?"

Mya chewed her lip as she tried to remember. Tried to see if there was a feeling inside of her that would tell her she had a mother, or a father. Even a brother or a sister. "I don't know."

"What about where you are from?"

She shrugged, biting her lip to stop the tears that threatened to fill her eyes.

"Your accent is different than this area. It's hard to tell where you are from. Maybe English? Or somewhere in Scotland near the border?" Doctor MacAslan wrote some more things down. "Boyle isn't a unique enough name to give you a territory. It could be Scottish, or even English. It could be a married name which wouldn't help tell us where you are from. We'll have to keep an open mind if there is news that someone is looking for you." He shook his head as he spoke to himself. He straightened suddenly and stood. "Have you had any pain in your head?"

"Like a headache?" She touched her forehead. "There's been a dull ache, but nothing sharp if that is what you are asking."

He nodded and moved close to her. "May I?" he asked and motioned to her head.

"Yes."

Doctor MacAslan pulled the loose bun from her hair and her auburn strands tumbled down, as if happy to be free. He felt along her scalp, checking with gentle, but expert, fingers. "No bumps or bruising. I don't see a blow to the head to indicate there may have been an accident." He stepped back. "You're a lovely girl. I can't see you disappearing unnoticed." He glanced down at her shoulder. "Unless it's for the better. Do you know who did this to you?" He pointed to the bad cut on her shoulder.

Mya shivered. Not from cold but from the realization of what the doctor was thinking. He believed someone had hurt her on purpose. Could that be why she couldn't remember? Maybe he thought she was running away. What if she was? "I don't know what happened." A tear slipped out of the corner of her eye and raced down her cheek.

Eleanora stood and handed her an embroidered handkerchief. She patted Mya's hand. "It's okay, dear. You don't need to figure anything out now. Or ever." She glanced at the doctor as if sending him a warning.

He nodded in understanding. "It may come back to you over time. Maybe in parts, maybe all at once." He shrugged. "Maybe never. Whatever is meant to be…" He turned and closed his notebook and gathered up his things. "I'd like to see you tomorrow again, Miss Bo—Miss Mya."

"No problem." Lottie stood. "We only want Mya to be safe. To be okay."

"Yes. I understand your concern."

Mya watched the three of them, sure there was part of a conversation going on that she was missing. "I'm not married. I'm sure of it," she said suddenly.

They all turned to look at her.

"Of course, dear." Lottie smiled kindly.

The doctor cleared his throat. "I shall drop by one morning soon, then," he said. "It seems you are doing fine. If anything arises, just sent for me. And make certain that there are no complications. No overdoing it." He turned to look at Mya. "You are a very lucky young lady. Such a wound could have easily done more damage than it did."

"I'm glad the damage wasn't much, then," Mya said, thankful the questions were over. "And I appreciate your help with it."

"As I said, it is no trouble at all. It's my job, after all, to look after the people of this town." He gathered up his bag, and tipped his hat to all of them. "Good day, ladies."

"Good day," they echoed.

"Well," Lottie said when he had gone, "that went quite well." She grinned at Mya. "Now that you know you won't drop dead if we let you leave the grounds, would you like to take a day trip with us tomorrow? We are headed to Inverness to do some shopping, and would rather not leave you here alone unless you have a preference for it."

"And if we are to get you some clothes that are not hand-me-downs," Eleanora added, "you will need to be fitted for them."

"That as well. So, what do you say?"

"If you do not mind taking me along," Mya answered. She hated that she had to have them pay for clothes for her. She would find a way to repay them. "I would love to visit the town with you."

Lottie clapped her hands together. "Excellent. We shall make a day of it, then. Shopping, lunch, and perhaps a walk down by the river before we return home in the evening, if you are not too tired."

Mya smiled. "Just you try and keep up."

The coach ride to Inverness from the estate was not a terribly long one, though the roads left a little to be desired. Mya, in a dress of Lottie's and a hat borrowed from Eleanora, leaned back against the seat as well as she could with the hat in the way and tried to ignore the jostling, despite the twinges of pain every bump sent through her shoulder.

When they arrived at the market, the coachman let them off, and Lottie stepped up to Mya's side, slipping an arm through hers as she had for the walk in the garden.

"Let's start here," she said, "and then later visit other parts of the city. The coachman will circle back around so that we can send our purchases with him periodically. Better that than lugging them all over Inverness."

"Just how many things do you intend on purchasing?" Eleanora asked from Lottie's other side, both eyebrows lifted.

Lottie shrugged. "Whatever catches my eye. The dry goods and such are already taken care of, but one never knows what exciting things one might find."

Shopping with Lottie, Mya discovered as they made their leisurely way through the covered market, was exactly what she might have expected. While the other woman had started out at her side, offering the support of an arm or a shoulder, she was quickly distracted, darting off to examine one thing or another almost constantly. Eleanora stepped in to take her place, a fond smile on her face even as she shook her head at Lottie's antics.

"Is she always like that?" Mya asked as they paused at yet another stall, Lottie talking animatedly to the shopkeeper as she turned a statuette over in her hands.

"Or worse," Eleanora said. "I think half of it is for show."

Mya turned away to hide a smile. It seemed she had been right the day before, when she teased Lottie about Eleanora's indulging her. She was fooling precisely no one.

"Though she is genuinely quite excitable, for lack of a better word," the blonde woman added as she and Mya followed Lottie to the next stall. "She takes a great deal more joy in life than most. It is a quality of hers that I rather wish I was better at emulating, however unfashionable it may be."

"That is—" Mya began, just as someone's shoulder knocked roughly against her own, making her stumble against Eleanora. "Excuse me!" she cried sharply, grabbing her injured arm.

The man who had nearly run her over stopped, turning slowly to look at her.

Mya's heart skipped a beat. He was gorgeous. His dark eyes swept over her, and Mya felt a sweet little shudder run down her spine.

"Your apology is accepted," he said.

It took Mya a moment to process the words. Her thoughts were caught on the way his voice sounded, deep and just a little rough, the kind of voice that would make any woman a little weak in the knees. At least, that was, until she caught up with what he had actually said.

"*My* apology?" Her eyebrows arched upward. "You're the one who ran into me."

"Mya," Eleanora whispered, voice so quiet that Mya doubted the man in front of them had even heard the quiet warning in the word.

He looked amused. "Is that so, lass?"

"I don't see how it could be interpreted otherwise."

For a moment, he simply stared at her, silent. A grin broke out across his face. "You are quite an usual specimen of femininity. Has anyone ever told you so?"

"And you are condescending and arrogant, but I suppose many have told you that."

"Mya!" Eleanora gasped beside her.

"Just what kind of scandalizing language are you using on poor Lord McGregor?" Lottie asked, appearing at Mya's elbow. "You've turned Ella completely red."

The man in question didn't seem at all perturbed by Mya. He was, in fact, laughing. Mya's jaw clenched. He was absolutely, insufferably annoying. The name, though, sounded familiar, and she wondered for a fraction of a second if she had known him before, only to remember that the name was one Eleanora had used the day before. Lord McGregor, the man who had found her in the back field. Mya felt her cheeks heat. The man who had likely saved her life. And here she was berating him on a public street. Not that he didn't deserve it.

"I am glad to see your encounter with that arrow doesn't appear to have dulled your spirits any, my lady," Lord McGregor said, bowing politely before straightening quickly.

Mya glanced down and then opened her mouth to answer him, but he was already gone, disappearing into the crowd. She snorted. Of course he had made thoroughly sure he had the last word. It was just the kind of thing a man like that would do.

"I cannot believe you spoke to Lord McGregor that way," Eleanora said, sounding as though she was not sure whether she wanted to be admonishing or impressed.

"Because he rescued me?" Mya asked. "Or because he has a title in front of his name?"

Lottie laughed.

"Both," Eleanora said. "Either."

"I spoke to him that way because he's a condescending ass," Mya pointed out to gasps from both of the other women. "And he completely deserved it. Running into me and then pretending as though I was the person who was in the wrong when he knew full well that it was his fault."

"Maybe he did not know," Lottie suggested. "Men can be rather oblivious."

"I think it's rather hard to be unaware of nearly stepping on a person."

"You would be surprised," Eleanora said, obviously speaking from experience in the matter.

"Either way." Mya shook her head. "I don't like him."

"The man saved your life, and you dislike him because he bumped into you at market." Unlike Eleanora, Lottie didn't sound conflicted. She sounded delighted by the whole thing, as though Mya had done something particularly thrilling.

When she put it that way, it did sound a little ridiculous, but she wasn't going to take the words back. "Yes."

"Living with you is going to be utterly fascinating." Lottie laughed, taking Mya's free arm. "I cannot wait."

They continued together through the market.

Chapter 4

The back field, Mya discovered, was a stretch of land at the foot of the hills that sloped up beyond the house. It was not landscaped the way the rest of the grounds were, only crossed by the tracks deer had worn through the vegetation. Lord McGregor, she was told, often walked there. Though it was Lottie's property, his land adjoined their own, and she did not mind him wandering through.

On a morning three days after their trip to Inverness, and her first encounter with the lord, Mya decided to take a walk there herself. Eleanora and Lottie were each in their studios, working on projects that she had no part in. Both had invited her to sit with them if she liked, but Mya found she was restless after the days of rain that had kept them all inside.

It was curiosity that led her back beyond the garden. Perhaps a rather morbid curiosity, actually. She wanted to see where she had been found before she had woken up in Lottie and Ella's guest room.

Finding the place, however, proved to be nearly impossible. There were no distinctive landmarks in the field beyond the occasional rock sticking up from the grass, and no one had told her any specifics. Some part of her had half expected to find a sign of some sort. Blood, maybe. Or grass trampled in odd patterns. But there was nothing. She had given up and was turning to make her way back to the house when a figure came over the rise ahead of her.

It had to be Lord McGregor, she realized almost instantly. Who else would be walking through Lottie and Eleanor's back field? Or someone as tall and roguishly handsome—even from far away. Mya briefly considered pretending as though she hadn't seen him and going on her way, but he had appeared so close to her that she was fairly certain he wouldn't be fooled. Before she could make a decision either way, he'd raised an arm and called a hello. Mya wondered if he thought she was one of the ladies of the house. It was highly doubtful that he had any interest in apologizing for his behavior at the market. Sighing, she waved back at him.

"Good morning, Miss Mya," he said as soon as he was close enough that he didn't have to shout.

"Lord McGregor," Mya said, only just verging on polite.

"I think, perhaps, we began wrong," he said.

"I wonder why that is," Mya retorted.

He laughed, a short, sharp bark of a laugh. "You are not like any woman I have ever met."

"And yet, you're exactly like every man I have ever met."

That wasn't strictly true. Mya had met a grand total of two men since waking up with no memory, and one of those men was Doctor MacAslan, who had been nothing but gentlemanly. But the sentiment felt real. Mya was sure she had known other men in her previous life, and the chances that at least a few of them had annoyed her as much as Lord McGregor did were high enough to gamble on.

The reply prompted another chuckle, and the sound of it settled low in Mya's belly, warming her from the inside out. Mya ignored the feeling.

"Laughing at me isn't going to convince me otherwise," she pointed out.

His eyebrows lifted. "If you are going to continue to look for things to be displeased with, I'm sure that you will find them, but might I suggest you stop and consider actually hearing what I am saying instead of immediately jumping at my throat?"

The reprimand stung. Mya lifted her chin, arms crossed over her chest, and stared him down. "I've heard what you are saying," she said.

"Yet you continue to behave in such a fashion. I thought I was doing you a favor, giving you an excuse, but I see now that you have none."

"Think what you like."

If he was going to lecture her, she was hardly going to remain and allow him to go on. She spun on her heel and started toward the house.

"Mya!"

She paused. Turned. He was standing closer than she had expected, near enough that she almost imagined she could feel the heat of his body against her own. Her throat felt suddenly tight. Her heart beat faster in her chest. "What?" she asked, forcing the word to come out flat.

"Are you truly going to walk away without so much as a word? I did save your life, you know."

Mya's fingers curled against her palms. "And just what does that have to do with this? Do you feel as though I owe you something for saving me?" she demanded.

"Of course not."

He sounded offended enough that Mya believed him. Still, she wondered what he'd meant by it. "Then why bring it up at all?"

"It is something a normal person might consider a good quality in another," he said, tone dry.

There was something about his voice, just then, the angle of the light on his face... Then it was gone. Mya shook her head. If they had known each other before her accident, he would have mentioned, surely. Unless there was something to be gained by keeping her in the dark. Maybe it wasn't luck that he had found her in the field.

But Mya dismissed the thought as quickly as it had come. Whatever she thought of him, he didn't seem like the sort of man who would be responsible for harming a woman.

"You can take a step back, now," she said.

One corner of his mouth curled upward. "Is that so?"

"It is so."

"And yet," he said, "here I am."

So close, he smelled faintly like ink and old paper, and beneath that of something warm and living. That too seemed strangely familiar, and Mya wondered if she was doomed to always be having flashes of familiarity that never resolved themselves into genuine memory, like a picture not properly developed. She found herself swaying forward, drawn toward him as though he exerted some physical pull.

His head tipped down. For the barest second, they almost touched, breath mingling warm between them.

Mya took a quick step back. Lord McGregor reached out, then stopped. His hand fell back to his side before it had even touched her. They stood for a moment, stock still, staring at each other, and then Mya turned and hurried back toward the house, feeling his eyes on her until the trees cut her off from his view.

Chapter 5

Mya walked barefoot under trees green with spring, their tender new leaves all unfurling toward the sky. The scent of coming rain curled around her, soft on the breeze, though the sun shone overhead, light spilling down through the branches to dapple the carpet of bluebells on the forest floor. In the murky green distance, a stag grazed among the silvery trunks. It stood bright against the green backdrop, its white fur almost shining in the sunlight shining directly on it.

Flowers brushed her, skin tickling against her feet. Mya took a breath, filling her chest with the sweet, elusive smell of them. It felt familiar, like something she had done before. The stag lifted his head, and their eyes locked.

Clouds that had not been overhead a moment before burst, and rain poured down, pattering through the leaves and soaking her to the bone. The stag bounded away.

She stood in the rain, watching it go, part of her wanting to chase after it.

Then suddenly, there were arms around her. A cloak lifted over her head to shield her from the rain. Laughing, she ran for the shelter of the house up ahead, and in a moment they were tumbling through the door, both of them dripping all over the floor. Mya turned to thank her rescuer, and found Lord McGregor, dressed not in the smart trousers and suit coat he had worn during both of their encounters, but in a kilt belted tight around his waist, his dark hair loosed from its tie and wet with rain. Water ran down the bare expanse of his chest, outlining the ripple of muscle. Mya traced the drops with her eyes, resisting the urge to lean in and lick them from his skin. When she lifted her gaze, he was watching her with knowing dark eyes and a smile on his face that made heat curl lazily under her skin.

He reached out, and the palm of his hand curved against her cheek, hot against her rain-chilled skin.

This time, when he leaned down to kiss her, she didn't turn and run.

She wrapped her arms around his neck, leaning up on her toes to press her lips to him in return, body melting against his chest. The hand that was not on her face curled around her hip, and then he was sliding both of his hands under her thighs, lifting her as though she weighed nothing, carrying her through to the room where she slept.

There was a rug there in front of the fireplace that she did not remember having been there before. He laid her down on the soft fur, and Mya ran her hands along the curves of his shoulders and down over his biceps, feeling the muscles there ripple under his skin as he undressed her. The clothes fell away as though they were as eager to leave her bare beneath him as she was to feel his skin against her own.

The world shifted, and they were both naked, the firelight skimming over their skin and dancing in Kayden's dark eyes. He leaned down and pressed his mouth to her throat, scattering kisses along the curve of it.

"Damn, Mya." Another brush of lips against skin. "You are so beautiful."

Mya's fingers curled in his hair as he worked his way down, pausing to lavish attention on her breasts, teasing her nipples with his tongue until she was panting, her back arched and her free hand clutching at the fur beneath her.

"Tell me you desire me," he said.

"I desire you," Mya answered, an echo she couldn't recall the source of. "I have wanted you since the moment we met."

His hand slid up her thigh, and she let her legs fall open under the push of it, her body aching for him.

"I want you, Kayden. Please. I want you."

He smiled. She felt the curve of it, pressed to the space between her breasts, and then he was moving down once more. Mya writhed under him, hips hitching upward. He pressed a hand against her belly to hold her still.

"Is this what you want, Mya?" he asked her, biting down gently on her hipbones, not yet leaning forward to taste her.

They had done this before. She was certain now. He had asked her that question, his hands against her and his mouth on her skin. But she could not follow the thread of memory; all her attention was focused on him. On his touch. On the teasing lilt of his words.

"Yes," she answered. "Yes."

He chuckled, low in his throat, and bent down to give her what she had asked for. At the first flick of his tongue against her, Mya abandoned all restraint, moaning and rocking into his mouth, gasping his name. The hand tangled in his hair tightened. She felt the hum of Kayden moaning into her when she writhed, crying out with the pleasure of it, and he quickened his pace, alternating between teasing her entrance and flicking his tongue relentlessly over her clit.

It was only a matter of moments before she was shuddering and coming beneath him, pleasure shocking outward through her veins and filling her up with light. He gentled her through it, fingers stroking her hip.

When she opened her eyes, he was leaning over her, weight propped up on one elbow and his hips rocking against hers, sending new sparks through already sensitized nerves. Mya rocked up to meet him, and then he was sliding in, filling her so perfectly, and they were moving together, the rhythm of their bodies at once familiar and new. Mya breathed in the scent of him and wrapped an arm around his neck, drawing him down into a long, slow kiss. His cock stroked over that perfect place inside her, and her thighs spasmed around him as she lifted her knees higher, opening herself to him. Her head tossed against the fur, hair spilling around her.

He reached one hand down to find her clit, rocking his thumb against it with the same rhythm his hips moved to. Mya bit back a cry, earning her a low, husky laugh. Pleasure coiled low in her belly again, wrapping her senses in its net. Her toes curled as she rode the wave higher, seeking the crash. Her vision blurred, and all she could think to do was keep moving, keep holding on. She reached for the ecstasy that waited, lingering on the edge of the fall. And then, suddenly, it was there. Heat washed from her head to the tips of her toes, her thighs squeezing hard around his hips, and a hoarse cry of his name escaped her lips.

Kayden groaned, buried his face in her neck, and bucked frantically up into her, holding on to her a little too hard as he rushed toward his own orgasm. He thrust hard one final time, groaning his pleasure, his head thrown back. She stroked his cheek, his shoulder, his back, and whispered words that she forgot even as they left her lips.

They lay together, then, panting, listening to the crackling of the fire in the hearth. Kayden's hand stroked through her hair. Her eyes lifted and met his.

"I love you," she said, and he laughed.

"And I you, Mya. My lovely one. Always and utterly."

The words were still ringing in her ears when she woke.

She lay there panting, strangely disappointed that it had only been a dream. Her racing heart felt naked without him. And she had no idea why.

Chapter 6

At breakfast the following morning, Mya felt as though Lottie and Eleanora would be able to read on her face what she'd dreamed about. Her cheeks felt constantly hot, burning with the memory of the dream. It had faded, somewhat, since the early hours of the night, but she could remember enough. She was certain that if she looked at them they would know she was hiding something, even if they couldn't guess what it was. Thank goodness Lord McGregor wasn't around; she'd die of embarrassment for sure.

Lottie, of course, knew right away. Mya thought Eleanora had likely noticed something was off and simply hadn't mentioned it. Staring intently at her food and not meeting anyone's eyes had likely not been the most subtle course of action, she had to admit to herself when Lottie got up from her own chair to drop lightly into the one beside Mya's.

"If you are attempting to hide from us," she said, "I believe you might be better served by not being in the same room."

A nervous giggle rushed up Mya's throat, too quickly to stifle. There was a moment of startled silence from Lottie. Slowly, not sure she even wanted to see the expression on the other woman's face, Mya lifted her head to find Lottie looking at her with one eyebrow lifted, her expression otherwise carefully blank. "I..." Mya looked down at her food again.

"Whatever it is, you can tell us," Lottie said. "We promise not to be scandalized." A smile slipped into her voice. "That is, I promise not to be scandalized. Ella promises nothing. She is constantly scandalized."

"Even if that had once been true," Eleanora retorted from across the table, "living with you, Lottie, has utterly ruined my ability to be anything of the sort." Her voice gentled. "Mya, dear, if you wish to talk about it, you may. If not, simply tell Lottie to mind her own business. She will not actually make you give up any information you would rather keep to yourself."

"That's true," Lottie said. "I will not."

Mya pulled her lower lip between her teeth, sighing. Of all the people in the world she might discuss the dream with, Lottie and Ella were hardly the worst options. And perhaps they would be able to give her some aid in how to deal with it. Preferably in such a way that she could avoid turning bright red any time she came within five feet of Lord McGregor.

"I had a dream," she said, the words coming up much softer than she'd meant to say them. She cleared her throat and tried again. "I had a dream of a rather... intimate sort. I suppose I find it rather embarrassing, truth be told."

Lottie leaned forward in her chair, eyes shining. "Is that all? I'm quite sure that you are not the only person who's had such dreams. Do not worry yourself about it. And you are welcome to tell it to me—to us—in as much detail as you like."

That reaction didn't surprise Mya at all. Eleanora's soft chuckle, however, did. Mya looked up at the other woman, wondering what it was she found so amusing.

"You need not be embarrassed about it," Eleanora said. "I wouldn't go announcing it to the world at large, but we two are not going to judge you for such things. As Lottie said, you are hardly the only person to have them."

The words were somehow more reassuring coming from Eleanora. Lottie, Mya expected to be completely unconcerned about the issue, but Eleanora appeared to be rather conservative in comparison. It was a relief to know that she was not going to be judged.

"Who was it about?" Lottie asked.

Mya felt her cheeks go hot. "It was—" She swallowed.

"You do not have to say," Eleanora remarked, shooting a warning look at Lottie.

She knew that she didn't, but Lottie's gaze was still fixed expectantly on her, and Mya found that she wanted to say the name aloud.

"It was about Lord McGregor," she admitted, looking away and trying to ignore the fact that her entire face felt as though it was on fire.

"Oh..." Lottie sat back in her seat with a dejected air. "Well that was completely expected."

Mya stared at her. And then she laughed. "Are you serious? That's all the reaction I get? 'Well that was expected'? I'm mortified, and you're... disappointed?"

"I would have been much more interested if you had said the dream was about Doctor MacAslan," Lottie said, eyes twinkling.

"You are a very odd specimen of human," Mya answered, shaking her head.

The conversation might have gone on, if the maid had not entered just then with a quick little curtsy and an envelope in her hand. "The mail, missus," she announced.

"Thank you, Mary," Eleanora said, reaching out to take the envelope.

Lottie turned away from Mya at last to stare at the letter in Eleanora's hand as the maid scurried out again. "What is it?"

"Give me a moment," Eleanora said, rising from the table to take a letter opener from the desk in the corner of the room. "And I will tell you." When she had slit the heavy envelope open, she drew out a piece of paper and scanned the contents. "It seems," she said, her eyes moving left to right, "that we are invited to a party in eight days' time."

"Whose party?" Lottie demanded, standing to move behind Eleanora and read over her shoulder.

"Mr. and Mrs. Auteberry. For their daughter."

"Hmm. Not the people I would have picked, but a party is a party." Lottie turned a smile on Mya. "You'll be coming with us, of course."

Mya didn't know how to argue with that. She was simply too grateful the conversation had been turned to another topic and she didn't have to go into detail about her dream that had felt so real.

It felt more like a memory than a dream. She pushed the thought aside, preferring to listen to Lottie talk about dresses and what they would wear.

Preparing for a party, as it turned out, was a lot more work than Mya would have expected, especially since they were not the hosts. But there were apparently dresses to be made, and corsets to be fitted. Gloves and shoes, along with hats to buy.

The days flew past in a blur of activity. At the same time, Mya's shoulder healed as the good doctor had said it would. She grew excited about the party and thankful that the doctor wasn't looking for her family. For some reason, it felt like everything she needed was close by. That there wasn't a family looking for her. He questioned her again about her memories, but didn't press her. Mya had the thought that the doctor assumed she'd run away and was pretending not to remember. She let him think that without a shred of guilt. She was sure her memory would come back eventually. Until then, she was going to enjoy the company of Lottie and Eleanor.

Lottie had found out most of the guest list, and spent some time each evening coaching Mya on who would be there. Most of the names were easily forgotten, the details about their owners not important enough to truly keep Mya's interest. She didn't see any reason to know everything about everyone at all times. Surely there were better, more relaxed, ways to handle socializing.

One guest, however, she did care about.

"Lord McGregor will be there, of course," Lottie said two nights before the party.

Mya paused in the middle of examining her reflection in the mirror, one of the new hats perched on her head. "He will?" she asked, trying to pitch the question in such a tone that it did not sound as though she cared.

Lottie, of course, saw right through it. "There, and, as far as anyone knows, still single. Things may not stay that way for long, unless I completely miss my guess, so if you want a chance I say take it before it is gone."

"Why would it not stay that way?"

"He is a very eligible bachelor," Lottie said, lounging across the bed with her hair undone and her shoes off. "He has quite an adequate salary, and of course his own estate. And it's hardly a stretch to call him handsome."

"I'm not actually looking to marry him, you know," Mya pointed out.

"No? What is it that you seek to do, then? Just get him in bed?"

Mya blushed instantly. She felt the heat in her cheeks and saw the color in her reflection in the mirror. "I think that is rather frowned upon, actually. I thought I would simply leave him be." Mya shrugged. "Just because I had a dream about the man does not mean that I need to start hearing wedding bells. I didn't like him when I first met him. I am not going to fawn all over him now."

"It is Kayden you ought to be trying that disinterested act on, not me."

Mya froze. "I-I beg your pardon? Did you say Kayden?"

"Yes," Lottie said, completely unaware of what she had just done. "Kayden McGregor. I thought we had told you his first name."

Mutely, Mya shook her head. What was she meant to say to that? That she had known it without being told? That would suggest that she had somehow known Lord Kayden McGregor before the accident, but that was impossible. He hadn't told her, and he hadn't known who she was. Yet, that wanton dream of hers had him calling his name. There had to be some other explanation.

Lottie remained a few minutes longer, trying to engage Mya in some other conversation about some of the attendees. Most of it was gossip. When all she got were single-syllable answers and the occasional nod, she gave up with a sigh and left Mya to herself, heading out to find Ella or someone else she could talk to.

When the room was empty, Mya sank down on the edge of the bed, running a hand through her hair.

She had known his name, in the dream. Maybe, she thought, she had heard it somewhere. From someone that she couldn't remember. Bits and pieces of her memory seemed to be coming back occasionally. Small things, like rolling hills of country side, a melody of a song she knew, things that were not helpful to who she was, but it was at least a start. Once in the carriage, there had been a view of the hillside that she swore she had seen before, except without the houses in it. Maybe it had been a painting or something, she wasn't quite sure. So she kept the thoughts to herself, not quite ready to share. She thought of Kayden again. Perhaps that name had just been lurking in the back of her mind. He was, as Lottie had said, quite rich. And his name was well known in the area. If she had come from a town nearby, which seemed likely, she would have heard it. The dream had simply supplied it when her conscious mind had not been aware enough of the information's existence for her to recall it outside of a dream.

That was it.

And yet, the explanation, no matter how much sense it made, did not satisfy the nervous knot in the pit of her stomach, or the question of why she felt as though she had known him when there was nothing to indicate that she had ever met him before the day in the market.

Chapter 7

The party, or somewhat of a ball as Eleanora called it, was being held on the other side of Inverness, at the estate of Mr. and Mrs. Auteberry. That meant a coach ride longer than the ones Mya had yet taken. She was grateful that her shoulder seemed to be nearly healed; the jolts of the coach over the ruts in the road hardly pained her at all.

"Now," Eleanora said as they rattled along. "Is there anything that you should like to know about proper manners in attending a party?"

She had already given Mya a rather basic explanation of the most important rules, some of which seemed incredibly silly. The rule about a woman not crossing the room at a dance without an escort had made Mya laugh, and Eleanora had shrugged when she asked why it was so terribly necessary. And odd that Mya didn't really know the rules of conduct. She should, shouldn't she?

"In truth," she had said, "I'm not particularly fond of it myself, always having a man hanging on my arm, but one does what one must in polite society."

Mya considered what she knew, and whether there was anything else that she ought to be aware of. It was difficult to gauge what she didn't know, considering that she didn't know it. And the more rules she knew, the more she would have to keep track of. If there were any that Eleanora had forgotten, Mya would let them stay that way, and truthfully plead ignorance if she failed in their execution.

"No," she said. "I'm sure there are things that I do not know, but I have enough rules running about in my head. If I learn any more there isn't going to be room for myself."

That earned a laugh from Lottie, and a smile from Eleanora.

"You have learned the most important ones, anyway," Lottie said. "All the little ones about how exactly to stand if a man asks you for a dance and if you wish to refuse him while there is another man within hearing distance, and the exact shape of the smile one should wear for every course of dinner, are not going to get you thrown out if you mistake them."

"Those are not truly rules," Mya said, chuckling. "They're just silly."

"No," Lottie agreed. "They are not rules. Though there is one about never accepting a dance from one gentleman immediately after turning down another. And a few others more rigorous than that. But as I said, they are not important tonight." She exchanged a glance with Eleanora, who smiled at her. "What is important," she added, turning back to Mya, "is enjoying yourself. That is what parties are for, after all, no matter how some people try to stifle them."

"Tell me something about Mr. and Mrs. Auteberry?" Mya asked.

In all their preparation for the party, she did not think the hosts had been mentioned in more than passing.

"They are quite wealthy," Eleanora said.

"And quite English." Lottie's tone was disparaging. "They have a daughter who is close to your age, I believe. They had her coming out party in London last Season, but of course they must introduce her here too, now that it is over. It seems she could not catch a man in London, and they are trying for a Scot."

"If the queen does something," Eleanora said, with more venom in her voice than Mya had ever heard from her, "everyone who is anyone must do it. Never mind that only decades ago the people of the Highlands were not allowed to wear our own colors or keep our own traditions. Now they scramble after an idea of it they do not even understand so they can impress those richer and more connected than they are with their awareness of the queen's whims."

For a moment, Mya was too surprised to come up with an adequate response. She might have expected that sort of commentary from Lottie, but Eleanora generally carried herself with an air of quiet contentment, only marred by the occasional moment of concern for another. Mya wondered now how much of herself she kept under wraps for the sake of propriety.

"If you do not like them, why accept the invitation at all?"

"Because if we do not make a certain number of social outings in a season they will start to wonder what we are doing, holed up in the house, and spend far too much of their time coming up with outlandish rumors to explain our absence," Lottie said. "And because there will be a great many people there whom I do enjoy seeing. And the Auteberrys do lay quite a table for dinner parties."

Eleanora laughed softly. "Valid reasons, all," she said.

"Do you ever throw parties yourselves?" Mya asked.

"Oh, no. Not for a very long time. We hosted a few when James lived, but I lost interest when he fell ill, and after that I never thought of one I should particularly like to host." Lottie looked thoughtful. "We might see about it, though. Perhaps I shall drag my old hostess skills out someday soon."

"When she hosted parties," Eleanora said with a proud smile, "they were legendary. People would not dream of missing a Lottie Alan ball."

"They were quite well done," Lottie agreed, her smile soft with nostalgia. "Yes. Now that you are with us, I will organize one. For your introduction to society."

"I would think this party would be introduction enough," Mya said.

Lottie shook her head, curls bouncing. "No, no, darling. If you are going to be introduced, it must be at a party hosted by those who know you, and can present you to the world as you ought to be presented. Not as simply another name called at an event for someone else."

"I thought you did not think much of coming out balls."

"I do not." Lottie gave her a conspiratorial smile. "But I will throw one if it is the best way to have a bit of fun."

As though to punctuate Lottie's declaration, the carriage rolled to a halt. A moment later, the footman was at the door, lending them each a hand to step down. Mya moved carefully, unused to the long gown and crinoline that kept threatening to trip her up.

It was, however, a lovely gown, and despite the constriction of the corset and the number of times she had nearly fallen over, Mya was rather proud of it. The pale green muslin looked good against her skin and the red of her hair, which Lottie had bound up in a chignon with gem-studded pins.

Lottie, of course, handled the skirts expertly, though she had protested before the party that she never wore such things if she could help it, and she would likely be completely out of practice. The deep red gown was cut daringly low, trimmed in black lace, and Mya caught more than one pair of eyes fixed on her as they moved past the other new arrivals and into the manor.

Eleanora's gown, too, was trimmed in black lace at the sleeves and neckline, but there the similarities stopped. The overskirt and bodice of the gown were midnight blue, set with panels of tartan in navy and green, pin-striped with yellow and red. She wore bluebells from the garden in her hair.

At the door, a footman took their names and handed them each a dance card, and as they stepped into the main ballroom, a butler announced their arrival.

"Miss Ottilie Alan," he called. "Miss Mya Boyle. And Miss Eleanora MacLaren."

Heads turned, and Mya felt eyes on them as they descended the flight of steps to the ballroom. A tall blonde woman whom Mya assumed to be the hostess was immediately at their elbows, dainty hand resting in the crook of her husband's arm.

"Such a pleasure to see you," she was saying. "We are so glad you could attend."

"Mrs. Auteberry," Lottie said. "Lovely to see you, as always. Mya, this is our delightful host, Mrs. Auteberry."

"I have heard so much about you," Mya said, giving a polite little dip of her head as Eleanora had instructed earlier in the afternoon.

"Likewise, Miss Boyle. And of course, Ottilie and Eleanora know my daughter, Blanche. Blanche, darling, this is Mya Boyle, a guest of Ottilie and Eleanora's."

"How do you do?" Miss Auteberry asked, performing the same neat little bow that Mya just had.

"Quite well," Mya answered, hoping she did not sound as stiff as she felt. "Thank you."

Miss Auteberry shared her mother's narrow frame and thin blonde hair, topped with a chaplet of daisies. She was dressed in pale pink gauze, trimmed with drapes of white lace, and her simpering smile was so obviously fake Mya wondered how much time she had spent practicing it in the mirror. Eleanora's equally false expression at least looked natural on her face to anyone who had not spent a fortnight living in her home. With Lottie, it was quite impossible to tell what was going on behind the wide and not at all demure grin she was wearing, though Mya knew just what her opinion of the Auteberrys was, and didn't envy them that opinion in the slightest.

"Miss MacLaren," Mrs. Auteberry said, beckoning a sallow young man with ears too big for his face forward from one of the clusters of people around them. "Mr. Bartholomew Smith."

Eleanora's smile went a little strained at its edges as Mrs. Auteberry hurried off into the crowd to introduce some other unlucky couple, the band striking up the music for the first dance. Lottie laid a hand on Eleanora's shoulder, and Mya saw her squeeze gently, a silent offering of support.

"My lady," Mr. Smith said, his accent obviously English. "I was wondering if you might be pleased to have this dance with me."

"I should not be, thank you," Eleanora said, turning away.

Mya watched the young man's shoulders slump. Lottie was leaning over, whispering something in Eleanora's ear and blatantly ignoring the little crowd of young men who had gathered at her back, apparently waiting to ask her for a dance. When she turned and found them waiting there a moment later, her eyebrows lifted.

"Yes?"

"Miss Alan," one of the bolder of the young men said, stepping forward and bowing at the waist. "I wished to ask you if you might grant me the honor of dancing the waltz with me."

Lottie and Eleanora exchanged a glance too quickly for Mya to read. "With pleasure, sir."

She turned a benevolent smile on the next young man in line. "Mya," she said, glancing around as she spoke. "This is Mr. Baird. Mr. Baird, Miss Mya Boyle."

"A pleasure," Mya said.

Mr. Baird, obviously aware of his newly assigned role in the little tableau Lottie had engineered, bowed. "Miss Boyle, might I have the pleasure of dancing the waltz with you?"

Mya sought Eleanora, who dipped her chin in a nod small enough that others would not notice it. She turned back to the red-haired Mr. Baird with a smile. "Gladly, sir."

He was not the man she wished to dance with, but he was rather attractive. A dancing round across the ballroom with him would not be a chore. Whether Mr. Baird would come to regret his offer when he learned how rudimentary her dancing skills were, was another matter entirely.

It was not that Mya could not dance at all. In the week leading up to the ball, Lottie and Eleanora had taught her most of the basic steps, Eleanora leading her through the movements and Lottie calling time and instructions from the side. But she had only had a little time to practice, and most of the women in the room had been dancing since they were girls. Her body had not seemed particularly inclined to recall the steps, though Lottie had told her that she must have danced sometime. If that was so, she had either danced different steps, or not danced well, because there had been no muscle memory of the dances they had taught.

Mr. Baird must not have regretted their dance too terribly; between him and Lottie, Mya was introduced to a number of young men, all of them politely asking for space on her dance card. By the time the band was striking up the third dance, her card was nearly full. Only the spots she had deliberately kept open were free. Lottie was in something of a similar situation, and had already turned away nearly a dozen prospective dance partners, each with a polite apology that she was already engaged. Eleanora had retired to the edge of the dance floor, where she was seated and talking with one of the other young ladies.

"There will be men over there asking them to dance soon," Lottie said, leaning in to speak the words softly enough that they would not be overheard.

From a quick glance around the room, it looked as though there were more women than men at the ball, and Mya was not so sure, but when she expressed the reservation, Lottie shook her head.

"One of the party hosts will ask, or send a friend to. They must make sure that every woman in the place dances, or the ball will not be seen as a success."

"That is rather kind of them," Mya said.

"Kind?" Lottie laughed. "It is an issue of social standing, for the most part, though there are a few who are genuine."

As she spoke, the third dance struck up, and their partners appeared to draw them apart and in for the dance. Mya noted, from the corner of her eye, that Eleanora had risen from her seat with the other young lady, and they were taking their places on the floor, opposite each other. She hid a smile behind her fan. A shortage of men, it seemed, wouldn't stop the women from getting to enjoy themselves. Another pair of girls had joined the line at Lottie's end.

The dance was a quick one, though it was not one of the ones Mya had struggled to learn. The steps were simple, and she enjoyed the energy of it. Skirts and curls were bouncing with the light motion of the dance, and she heard beneath the music the occasional soft peal of laughter or delighted cry ring out. She would glance every so often around the room, or toward the entrance and then back to the dance floor. As she wove in and out of the line of dancers, she caught sight of Lottie, who was swinging a turn on the arm of her partner, dark hair flying and eyes alight. Eleanora, for the moment in the arms of one of the men, whose partner was temporarily engaged with another before the motion of the dance brought them back together, was laughing along with the rest of them.

When the music slowed at last to a stop, they were standing as they had been at the beginning, facing their partners across the small space that separated the two lines. Everyone was breathing a little harder, faces flushed with exertion and enjoyment. Mya, glancing around the room once more, could understand, then, why Lottie was so intent on attending parties. They were far more pleasant than she had anticipated, given the number of rules that went along with preparing for them.

Lottie slipped the gaze of her escort and laid a hand over Mya's arm, leaning against her shoulder. "Did you enjoy yourself?" she asked as Eleanora came up on her other side, a genuine smile still lighting her face.

"I think that one was my favorite," Mya said, getting a grin and a nod of agreement.

"I think that is the favorite of most young people," Eleanora said. "Though some of the older ladies and gentlemen are equally as fond of it."

"Do you need something to drink?" Lottie asked.

A drink did in fact sound nice, and they were making their way to the refreshment room when the butler called out a new arrival.

"Lord Kayden McGregor!"

Mya turned to look up toward the top of the steps, where Kayden, in a closely tailored charcoal gray suit, was making his way down. She thought the flush in her cheeks might not be entirely from dancing any longer.

That was confirmed when Lottie nudged her side.

"The man you were waiting for?" she teased.

"I was not waiting for anyone," Mya protested, to no avail. Her companions were obviously convinced that Mya had been on the lookout for Kayden's arrival. Which, if she were honest, was not entirely untrue. Though she had not been pining for him. Only wishing to see if he would show up. And see what he would look like dressed in fine clothes. Or if he would wear a kilt, like her dream. And if he was a fine dancer? And if he would ask her to dance. No, she had not been pining for him at all.

"As you are already introduced, it will not violate etiquette for him to ask you if you would like a dance. Give it a few moments and we shall see what he does."

"He will have to dance with the young lady of the household first," Eleanora said, brushing a loose wisp of hair back from her face. "But I think that will not be a recurring activity."

Mya, watching as Kayden was presented to the hosts of the ball and a smiling Blanche Auteberry, hoped it would not be. A spike of jealousy flickered through her. Strange, as she had no ties to Lord McGregor. She found him insufferable to say the least.

The next dance was not one on the card, and Mya looked to Eleanora and Lottie to explain. Lottie rolled her eyes.

"It's not acceptable to cancel on a dance partner who has signed your card," she said. "But the unscheduled dances are open to choice. So, they have given Miss Auteberry the opportunity to dance with Lord McGregor by slipping an extra dance in. It's manipulative, but not considered rude, as there will be a few dances over the course of the night that are not on the card. They can claim this is merely the moment the band chose to slip one in."

Miss Auteberry was, in fact, dancing with Kayden. Mya, rather than take an invitation, begged out on the excuse that she was not used to such exertion after a recent convalescence and retired to a chair along the wall to watch.

He was a beautiful dancer. And not only in the sense that he was a beautiful man. Watching him was spellbinding, every motion smooth as a hunting cat's stride. Mya could almost see the way the muscle shifted under the close-fitting cloth of his suit as he led a rather clumsy Miss Auteberry across the floor.

Heat rushed to her face, and Mya lifted her fan, attempting to cool the red blush that must be sitting on her cheeks at the memory of the dream, suddenly vivid in her mind's eye.

"Are you well?" a voice asked beside her. "Do you need air, or perhaps water?"

"Oh," Mya said, turning to face the young woman who was leaning worriedly over from the next seat. "I am quite well. Thank you. Just a little unused to so much dancing." She smiled. "Hello. I am Mya Boyle."

"I—" The girl giggled a little. She was on the plain side, her dress of a less quality fabric than some of the finer ones in the room, but her brown eyes were very pretty, and the little gap between her two front teeth made her smile rather sweet. She seemed the kind of person that it would be pleasant to have a conversation with. "I do not think you are meant to do that."

"Do what?"

"Introduce yourself. Without, well, a host. Or someone."

Mya did not point out just how ridiculous she thought that rule was, though she really wanted to. She shrugged, and offered a smile. "I will not tell if you won't."

There was no one close enough to hear, and they could always claim later that they had met properly. The young woman smiled.

"Very well, then. I am Agnes Donald."

"I am delighted to meet you, Agnes," Mya said honestly.

By the time Lottie and Eleanora returned from the dance, Mya had discovered—while watching Kayden from the corner of her eye—that Agnes was the youngest of four daughters, and that her dress had been passed on from the one above her in age. Her family was well off enough to make into the upper echelons of polite society, but only just, which left her unsure of where she fit in the scheme of things. Mya thought perhaps making friends with a pair of eccentric, wealthy young women might help in that regard. Of course, it might also do more harm than good. It all depended on how eccentric one considered Lottie and, by extension, Eleanora. Her brusque dismissal of the young man earlier in the night had likely not aided her case.

"Miss Donald, is it?" Lottie said when she had reached them, dismissing the young man who had escorted her across the floor to her seat. "How lovely to see you again."

"Miss Alan," Agnes said, dipping her head in a little bow. "And Miss MacLaren," she added as Eleanora too was dropped off at her seat by a dance partner who seemed to sense rather quickly that his presence was no longer desired.

"Hello, Miss Donald," Eleanora said, offering a kind smile and smoothing out her skirts. "Mya, who is next on your dance card?"

Mya glanced down at the little booklet hanging from her wrist. "There is an empty space," she said. She had left it in the hopes that Kayden, or at least someone more interesting than the vapid boys who flocked after Lottie, might ask her.

"I think you will soon find it filled," Lottie said, grinning at her.

As though the words were prophecy, Kayden appeared through the crowd, headed their way. Mya could not bring herself to think of him strictly as Lord McGregor, though she knew that she ought to, considering his station was well above her own, and a slip as intimate as calling him by his given name after only two meetings might well start the kinds of rumors that were very difficult to stop. But Lord McGregor just felt...wrong. Kayden was the name that kept sighing across her thoughts and echoing in her dreams. Just Kayden.

"Miss Boyle," Kayden said when he was standing between them and the milling group on the dance floor. "Miss Donald." He dipped his head to each of them in turn. "Miss Alan. Miss MacLaren."

"Lord McGregor," they greeted, more or less in chorus.

He swept into a bow. "I was wondering, Miss Boyle, if I might have the honor of dancing with you at your next available convenience."

"With pleasure, Lord McGregor," Mya said. "That convenience is, in fact, now. No one asked me to dance the Schottische."

That was not strictly true, but it was likely better than admitting that she had turned away more than three prospective dance partners in order to leave the slot open. That was not the kind of behavior considered acceptable in polite society, and she well knew it.

"Then I shall be glad to escort you to the dance floor," Kayden said with a handsome smile.

He straightened, and Mya rose, only to pause as he turned and bowed to Agnes. "Miss Donald," he said. "Perhaps I might be permitted the pleasure of dancing with you after this round?"

Agnes giggled, her cheeks turning pink. "I would be more than happy to give you a dance, Lord McGregor," she answered, her voice fluttery despite her best efforts to keep it under control.

As they turned away from the little group of women at the edge of the room, Mya smiled. "She will remember that for a long time to come."

"I am only doing what is expected of me," Kayden said.

Mya almost stumbled as her feet momentarily stopped moving and the rest of her body went on without her. Just doing what was expected. Her jaw tightened. "Is that all it is, then?" she asked as they promenaded onto the dance floor. "Doing what is expected?" She looked up at him. "Do you take no joy in it at all?"

"No more than the joy of something right done well."

She ought to have known better than to accept his invitation. Condescending arse. They would see how much joy he got out of it when she stepped all over his toes.

Chapter 8

"If you say that to Agnes," Mya said as the dance began, "so help me, I will find a way to push you down the hill behind Lottie and Eleanora's house. Head first."

Kayden's eyebrows lifted, the corner of his mouth quirking up in a smile that wasn't sure yet whether or not it ought to appear. "Say what to Agnes, for heaven's sake?"

"That rot about only doing it because it's what is expected of you and the joy of something right done well. It'll make her cry, and I will hate you for that."

"Rather a strong opinion over nothing more than proof that I am a well-mannered man," Kayden said, his voice curt.

Mya trod rather heavily on his toe. He startled backward, obviously surprised that she had done such a thing, and almost stumbled into the couple behind him. His eyes narrowed as he stared down the bridge of his nose at her. "Was that purposeful?"

"Purposeful?" Mya looked up at him with an innocent expression copied wholesale from Lottie. "I have only had less than a week to learn how to dance. And I have just come off *more* than a week of convalescence following an arrow to the shoulder. Which, might I add, you found and therefore certainly know about. It is hardly my fault I am a terrible dancer. I don't ever remember dancing before this." She stepped on his toes again. It was the perfect dance for it; there was a great deal of skipping about.

"I have danced with cows more graceful than you are," Kayden said, the hand on her hip tightening as they spun together, lifting her half off her feet for a moment so that she was hardly standing on them. Mya viciously ignored the little sparks of warm desire that his easy display of strength sent racing along her spine. She was not going to think about how she desired him. Or the dream. And she was absolutely not going to allow him anything more than the single dance that she had agreed to give. When that was done, it would be goodbye and good riddance.

"If you are so lacking in interesting female company that you are practicing your romantic overtures on cattle, I think it is you, and not I, who are troubled."

She wished she had the proper angle to accidentally stick an elbow in his ribs.

What was expected of him indeed. Poor Agnes.

And as for herself, well, she had known from the beginning that he was hardly deserving of her time. She would finish her dance with him and move on, and later she and Lottie and Ella could laugh at his ridiculous pompousness. It didn't hurt her one bit that he felt the need to behave as though the entire world revolved around his will, and his deigning to notice those beneath his feet was a magnanimous gesture.

"What exactly is it that you dislike about me so?" Kayden demanded.

"For one, you are utterly conceited," Mya said. "And for another, I cannot believe you would ask me to dance and then act as though I am, at best, some kind gesture you are making for the good of your social life!"

The words were a little louder than was perhaps prudent, and Mya saw more than one head turn. Kayden said nothing, and eventually the nearby dancers went back to their own business.

"When did I say that?"

"When you stated that you find no joy in dancing and consider it only doing a good deed. Offering social aid to the plain and dull, or whatever it is you believe that you do."

Kayden stared at her. "I did not mean you," he said finally. "What on earth would make you think that?"

"The fact that you said it behind the back of the next woman you invited to dance with you, directly to my face. And then you act like this, as though the fact that it is apparently only Agnes you are prepared to talk about that way makes it somehow better, or not worthy of judgment."

"I simply—" Kayden cut himself off with a low growl of frustration. "What I mean, Miss... Miss... Mya—"

"It's Boyle. Miss Mya Boyle," she hissed.

"What I meant, *Miss Boyle*, is that, like it or not, most men are not going to dance with Agnes Duncan. That is not my fault. But I will do something about it if I can, as will the other gentlemen here. The point of such a party is that everyone is welcome, and we wish to make them feel that way. I did not intend for you to take some kind of message from it that we are heartless heathens who see every girl we are not interested in throwing ourselves in bed with as social capital. Do a good deed, get a cake, or whatever it is that you believe. And most of what I meant, in fact, is that I did not feel the need to accept praise for simply doing the right thing. Thus your comment about her remembering my noble deed was unnecessary."

"Oh. Well then," she huffed, "I can see now that I was wrong. So generous you are, and humble as well. Truly a catch."

"Once again, you are looking for things to be angry about."

"It is hardly a difficult search."

That, at last, seemed to shut him up. They danced the rest of the piece in silence punctuated by the occasional hiss from Kayden when Mya stepped on one of his feet. It took some effort not to laugh at that.

When the dance was done, Kayden delivered her back to the edge of the room and picked up Agnes, taking her by the hand and giving Mya a very pointed look as they disappeared into the crowd. Mya crossed her arms over her chest and watched them move together, Agnes practically glowing with a smile. Whatever Kayden's motivations, she did have to admit that he had given

Agnes something to be happy about. At least someone had a positive experience.

When she realized she was sitting and sulking, Mya levered herself up out of the chair and turned her back on the dancers, slipping unnoticed out of the ballroom and down the hall toward the ladies' dressing chambers and the refreshment room, both of which seemed like better places to be rather than watching Kayden and Agnes laugh together.

There was some rule, she rather vaguely recalled, about chaperones, but the whole thing was frankly ridiculous. She was capable of walking down a hall on her own. It was hardly as though some barbarian murderer was going to leap out from behind one of the draperies and stab her in the middle of the Auteberrys' fashionable home.

As she passed one of the halls that led down another direction, she heard the sound of whispering, and took a quick step back, peaking around the turn of it. She was surprised to see Eleanora and Lottie standing halfway down, leaning in toward each other and conversing in voices too low for her to make out words. Ella looked upset about something, and Lottie was obviously trying to comfort her, catching one of her hands and holding it as she leaned in nearer to say something a little less urgent and a little gentler.

"—was deliberate," Eleanora said, loud enough that it startled Mya into darting back out of view. Her volume dropped again, though not quite as low as it had been before. "She knew what she was doing, Lottie, and I would sooner—"

"Hush," Lottie said. "Yes. She knew, but there is hardly anything to be done about it now. Do not let it ruin the night for you when it has otherwise been such fun."

Her voice grew more distant as she went on, and when Mya worked up the courage to poke her head around the corner again, she found the hall empty, both of them gone back to the dance floor, or the dressing room. She decided to let them be, and perhaps obtain something to settle the edge of hunger that dancing had provoked.

The refreshment room was empty when she arrived there, and Mya helped herself to a few cookies, nibbling at one with nuts and berries in it. It was better than she had expected. She finished it quickly, and the second cookie followed right after. She was reaching for a third when she heard footsteps coming down the hall. Guilt hit her. Lottie and Eleanora were taking care of her and Eleanora had been upset about something. Now here she was, chaperone-less. She realized that she could get Lottie and Eleanora in trouble if she was found ignoring the rules. She ducked back against the wall beside the open door and hoped that the sounds were just one of the servants going about his business, and that his business didn't include the refreshment room.

No such luck.

The footsteps turned, and entered, and belonged to Kayden. Blessedly, he had not yet seen her, his back still to the door and her little corner. Mya tried to edge silently out of the room before he turned. But of course, she had only managed half the distance when Kayden spun to face her, his eyebrows lifting.

"Are you hiding from me now?" he asked, laughter at the edges of the words.

"Not in the slightest," Mya snapped back, brushing imaginary wrinkles from her skirt with both gloved hands. "I simply thought I would remove myself from the room before I was required to engage in further conversation with you."

"Am I truly that terrible? That you will not even speak to me?"

Mya was surprised to hear the genuine concern in his voice. She took a breath, opening her mouth to speak, and closed it again. "No," she said finally. "It's not that. I was concerned about breaking rules by being in the hall alone. I would not want to get Lottie and Eleanor in trouble with the hosts."

"I'm not sure being in the hall alone with me is any better," Kayden said, sounding almost devilish. He smiled, his dark eyes warm in a way that made Mya's knees feel like one of the partially melted ices sitting on the table. "In truth, I think it may be worse, as far as the hosts are concerned."

He took a step forward, toward her, and Mya took a breath she forgot to let out again. She didn't like him, she reminded the part of herself that was melting into want at his approach. He was arrogant. And condescending. And the fact that he was handsomely gorgeous did not change any of that. It didn't.

But when he closed the last distance between them and brushed the backs of his knuckles tenderly over the curve of her cheek, Mya didn't pull away. She leaned into the touch, breath escaping in a sigh.

The touch felt so strangely familiar. So perfectly right.

He leaned down and kissed her, and Mya forgot her objections about his character entirely.

Voices in the hall made them startle apart an instant later, Mya's cheeks burning red as a signal light. Anyone who walked into the room in that moment was going to know exactly what had happened. They might as well have shouted it. But no one came in. The footsteps receded onward down the hall, and Mya slipped out the door and back toward the noise of the ball before Kayden could stop her. By the time she arrived back at the edge of the ballroom, all traces of what she had been up to in the corridor were gone.

"Well," Lottie said in the early hours of the morning as the coach rattled back down the road toward home. "You have had your first ball. Was it everything you dreamed that it might be?"

Mya, half asleep already despite the constant bumping of the wheels over rocks and into potholes, blinked her eyes open.

Lottie was sprawled across more than her share of the seat opposite, with her head resting on Eleanora's shoulder, regarding Mya through half-lidded eyes like a pleased and sleepy cat.

"It was not quite what I expected, actually."

"In what way?" Eleanora asked, genuine curiosity in the question.

"It was more exciting, I think." Mya smiled "After all the rules, I thought most of the entertainment would come from throwing those who broke them out of the house."

Lottie laughed. "They save that particular attraction for holidays. It would be rather expensive to keep it up indefinitely."

"Though..." Mya looked down at her hands, not sure that she could get through telling her story with a straight face if she raised her head to find Lottie staring at her. "I did threaten to kick Kayden McGregor down the hill."

"Lord McGregor? Whatever for?" Lottie asked

"When he invited me to dance with him, and then invited Agnes after, I told him she would remember that for a long time." Mya's voice tightened. "He told me that he was just doing what was expected of him, and that he found no more joy in it than any good man finds in doing what is required. I told him he had better not say that to Agnes."

"Are you sure he meant it the way you took him to?" Lottie asked.

"Does it matter?" Mya asked.

Eleanora and Lottie both looked at her across the interior of the carriage in silence.

Mya sighed. "He said that he meant I shouldn't praise him for doing something that was simply good manners. But I think that's nonsense. He meant that he didn't actually want to dance with Agnes."

"That is part of the ball," Eleanora said. "Gentlemen make sure that all of the ladies get to dance, whether they want to dance with that particular woman or not. Would you rather they were simply ignored? Left to sit alone with no attention?"

"No! But I don't think he needed to be saying things like that where she might hear them. Isn't making certain the women don't know that they were chosen out of duty rather than interest part of the etiquette?"

She vaguely remembered one of them saying something of the sort.

"Yes," Eleanora said. "It is."

"Do you know that when you are upset, you start to speak more like you did when you first came to us?" Lottie asked, leaning forward a little in her seat.

Mya's eyebrows drew together as she turned to look at the other woman. "What do you mean?"

"Contractions. Saying things such as 'don't' and 'isn't.'"

Actually, Mya hadn't realized. She shook her head. "No. I did not know that."

"It intrigues me, to be completely honest," Lottie said. "It is a lower-class habit, using them." She held up a hand to forestall Mya's denial before she could speak it. "I am not saying that I would judge you for such a thing, if it were true. It simply makes me wonder where it is you come from. Your accent, in general, is a bit different to others. There is something... traveled in it, perhaps. An interesting contradiction."

Mya had known that she had a slightly different way of speaking than the rest of them. She hadn't realized that others had noticed, though. She supposed it didn't actually matter, though she would have to watch herself around company. Lottie and Eleanora might not care that she had not come from a wealthy family, but other people would.

When they arrived at the house, Mya wished the other women good night and returned to her own room. It was tempting, as the night outside began to give way to the first light of dawn, to collapse fully clothed onto the bed, but she suspected she would regret falling asleep in a corset, and ruining the gown would hardly be a proper "thank you" for the amount of money Lottie had paid for it.

There was a maid, but Mya didn't want to wake her so late. Or rather, so early. Chances were, she would have to be getting up soon anyway, and Mya wasn't going to disturb the little bit of sleep she would have left. Which meant undressing herself. Not an impossible task, but one more difficult than she would have preferred after hours of dancing.

Something knocked against the window. Mya startled, turning to look out over the dim, gray landscape. The tap came again, on the side where the French doors opened onto the lawn. Mya turned, and pressed a hand over her mouth to muffle the sound that wanted to escape.

There was a man waiting outside the door.

A man, she realized, who had to be Kayden. As she approached, his form became clearer in the light spilling through the glass, resolving itself into the man she had expected to see. A sigh of relief rushed from her.

"What are you doing here?" she demanded as she opened the door. "You nearly frightened me to death!"

"I had to see you," he said. "I could not wait."

He leaned down and pressed his mouth to hers.

Chapter 9

There was a part of Mya that worried, even as she sank against Kayden's chest and arched into the kiss, that they would be discovered.

That part was very distant.

The rest of her was consumed with Kayden, the way his arms felt wrapped around her waist and the way his lips pressed against hers. She breathed in the scent of him and forgot entirely that air was a necessary thing.

When they at last broke apart, both of them were breathing harder, and Kayden was grinning like a fool.

"I'm glad I did not wait," he said, and then he drew her in again.

The second kiss was slower, gentler this time. He explored every inch of her mouth, his hands sliding over her body as they breathed in each other's air.

Mya's knees threatened to give out under the onslaught of sensations. It felt like she'd been waiting to kiss him forever. His muscular body seemed every inch as strong as she had dreamt it would be. His tongue seared a blaze inside of her that awoke her very core.

Their kiss broke, but Kayden did not let her go. The hand on her hip was curled around the curve of her corset, holding her close. She could still feel the warmth of his breath against her lips, the heat of his skin pressing through cloth.

"You look enchanting tonight," he said, his voice husky and low. "I meant to tell you so, before you decided that I was no longer acceptable company."

"I didn't want us to get caught," Mya said, her cheeks heating—from the compliment or their intimate position, she wasn't sure. "If we'd been noticed, there would have been gossip, and I have Lottie's and Ella's reputations to think about as well as my own. I'm not going to repay their generosity by ruining their public images."

Kayden laughed. "You are so very earnest. But I hardly think Lottie and Ella have any great concern about their reputations. Or did you not hear about Eleanor's little moment tonight?"

"If you're talking about her turning down that dance offer," Mya said, "I was there. Turning down a man for a dance, even if it is done in a somewhat rude manner, is not nearly as bad as being caught kissing in the refreshment room."

"And yet, we were not caught. So there's no need to worry." He smiled, and it had a wicked edge. Mya took a tiny step back, already feeling overly warm. "I will tell you something else, as well."

"And what is that?"

"That being caught kissing in the refreshment room is not nearly as scandalous as being caught naked in your bed with me."

Mya laughed. "Is that how you think this is going to go, then?"

"That is exactly how I think it is going to go," Kayden said, taking another step forward. She matched it with a step back. "If you had not wanted me here, you would never have opened the door."

"I could still tell you to leave," Mya pointed out.

"You could," Kayden agreed. "But would you?"

The next step had the back of Mya's legs pressed against the bed. Kayden moved forward another, and then the next, until he was standing almost pressed against her body. Mya sat down on the edge of the mattress, skirts spilling around her.

"You are wearing far too many clothes," he said.

"I am aware of that, thank you."

Kayden laughed, and reached for the pins that held her hair up, slowly pulling them free and dropping them on the bedside table one by one. "There are ways around that," he said, when he had finished and the copper locks were loose around her shoulders.

"Ways around clothes?"

He grinned wickedly at her. "Would you like me to show you?"

"I think I am quite aware of how—" She didn't have time to finish before Kayden had gone to his knees in front of her. The words caught in her mouth, her throat suddenly dry.

"Yes?" he prompted, eyebrows lifting.

"You are absolutely insufferable, I hope you know," Mya said, noting the lack of conviction in her own voice.

Kayden ignored her, sliding his arms under her skirts and lifting them up over his shoulders to disappear beneath them. Heat coiled slowly in Mya's stomach as she watched him, and then felt him.

One of Kayden's hands, big and warm, slid up her thigh, slipping under the fabric that covered her to rub the bare skin above her garter. Gooseflesh ran down her arms and prickled her skin. Was he truly going to do what she imagined he was about to?

The answer, it seemed, was yes, because his hand was moving again, and then he was dragging her undergarments out of the way and sliding his tongue up the length of her sex.

Mya's head fell back, her hands curling in the fabric of her skirts, and she stared up at the ceiling without seeing it, her entire body shuddering with pleasure. He seemed to know just the right places to drive her mad with it, and she wondered a little jealously how many other women's skirts he had been beneath. The thought was eclipsed by the reality of his mouth on her, his tongue stroking over her. His hands on her thighs, holding them open for him.

"Kayden!" Mya gasped, hardly louder than the sound of a breath.

She thought she heard him chuckle, muffled by the skirts and her thighs, felt the vibration of the sound against sensitive flesh. A moan escaped her. It occurred to her to be grateful that there was no one else in the guest wing of the house.

No one to hear the increasingly loud sounds he was coaxing from her throat.

Mya's thighs trembled against his shoulders, muscles drawing tight. Kayden must have known she was close, because the flicks of his tongue against the little nub of pleasure at the apex of her sex came faster.

"Kayden," she said again, breathless and shaking, fighting the embrace of the corset for air. "I—"

The words faltered and failed as the pleasure that had been coiling in her core exploded outward, racing up her spine and down her limbs, filling her whole body with heat. Colors danced across the backs of her eyelids. She might have cried out. The sound rang in her ears. His mouth gentled, and then stopped, one of his hands rubbing circles over her thigh.

When she slowly opened her eyes, Kayden was leaning over her where she'd collapsed onto the mattress and wearing a smile that was entirely too pleased with itself.

"You are a menace," Mya said, the words heartfelt, if still a little shaky.

"Are you telling me you wouldn't like me to do it again?"

"Clouds in heaven," Mya groaned. "If you do it again, I think I shall die."

He laughed, then. His smile clearly proud of what he had done to her. He had obviously enjoyed it as much as she had.

Giggles welled up in Mya's chest, and she had no choice but to let them free, still giddy with her recent release.

"I would hate to be the death of you," he said, sinking down to sit on the edge of the bed beside her and stroking his hand over the curve of her waist. "You will not be nearly so much fun if you are dead."

"What an accolade. I am most honored by your—"

Kayden cut her off with a kiss, leaning down and pulling her to him with a big palm cradling the back of her head. The kiss was long, and slow, and the perfect companion to the glow of pleasure that still hung over her. Mya stopped attempting to be witty, and just sank into it with a moan.

"You talk too much," Kayden said against her mouth, voice soft and teasing.

"So I have been told," Mya answered, and nibbled at his lips, wanting him to kiss her again.

Slowly, his weight sank down against her, and his palm curved against her cheek, guiding her where he wished her to be as his tongue claimed her mouth. Mya was more than willing to go along with that plan.

"If I do not get you out of these clothes in a moment," Kayden said when they paused for air, "I am going to have to pay for ruining them."

"Then get me out of them," Mya said, giving him a grin as he pulled back to look down at her. "You have hands."

"I ought to leave you here like this, just for that."

"Ah." Mya laughed, looking pointedly at the rather pronounced bulge in his trousers. "But I am not the one who is desperate."

"Minx," Kayden accused, though it sounded complimentary at the same time.

He took her hand and pulled her to her feet, spinning her around before she had time to steady herself. She might have stumbled had it not been for his hand on her shoulder, holding her up.

"Confound these things," he mumbled as he began working on the fastenings of her gown. "Why must they be so impossible to get out of?"

"For exactly this reason, I think," Mya answered, swallowing a laugh in case it might prompt him to actually follow through on his threat. "They do not want you despoiling innocent young ladies."

"Innocent, indeed. I do not think I imagined that you are just as eager as I am."

Mya did laugh, then. Kayden made a frustrated sound at her back, just as he managed to actually succeed in his task and get the gown to slide from her shoulders.

"Now you have to lift it off," Mya instructed.

"I am aware of how clothing works, my dear."

"Not that I have seen thus far," Mya retorted.

"Unbelievable." Kayden laughed as he lifted the gown over her head, tossing the whole thing in a rumpled pile on the bed. "I treat you like a queen and you do nothing but abuse me."

"Perhaps you need to be taken down a peg." Mya unfastened the straps that held the crinoline in place and let it fall, folding in on itself as it went. Then she gathered it up and laid it and the dress in the chair by the window.

"Clothes, clothes, and more clothes." Kayden sighed. "I swear they aim to convince men that there is not a human form at all under all that fabric."

"That is one way to protect women's virtue. Make it entirely not worth the bother."

Kayden's eyes slid slowly over her body, now hidden only by the most basic undergarments, and Mya felt the look like a touch. "You will always be worth the bother," he said, voice dropping low and husky.

Mya's cheeks went pink, but she didn't give him the satisfaction of fluttering about. "Flattery will not help you here."

"No?" Kayden's fingers began loosening the stays of her corset. "I think it has performed rather nicely thus far."

It was an unimaginable relief to let her ribs expand. The corset was not such a terribly uncomfortable thing as she had expected it to be when Lottie and Eleanora had introduced her to it, but there were moments at which she had wondered if dancing in such a contraption was an entirely wise choice. Little wonder some of the women had come so near fainting after some of the more vigorous numbers.

He turned her, and opened the fastenings up the front of the corset, catching it as it fell and laying it in the chair with the other things.

Mya took a deep breath and let it out again on a pleased sigh.

"Glad to be rid of it?" Kayden asked, the smile on his face saying he knew quite well that she was.

She didn't answer. Only reached down and pulled the chemise she had been wearing beneath it over the top of her head.

Kayden's eyes darkened as she threw it aside, not bothering with the chair for it. He stepped back into her space, curling his hands beneath the weight of her breasts and brushing his thumbs over her nipples. Mya gasped as they peaked under the touch. Her ribs and stomach were marked with the indentations the corset's boning had left behind.

Kayden ran his hands along them, and she shivered with the ticklish sensation of the barely there contact.

When his fingers reached her waist, Kayden stripped the drawers off, and Mya kicked them to the side, left only in her stockings and garters. She reached to loosen them, and Kayden stilled her hand.

"Those stay," he said, lips tilting into a crooked smile.

"Oh, they do, do they?" Mya's eyebrows lifted. "And what if I wish them to go?"

"Then you will break my heart," he replied instantly.

She laughed, and left the garters alone.

Kayden lifted her, hands around her waist, and set her on the bed. Mya leaned comfortably back on her hands, relishing the warm air of the room sliding over her naked skin. He, of course, did not have nearly so much clothing to remove as she had, and it was a matter of only moments before he was naked entirely.

He looked the way he had in her dream. Not just a little, as though she had guessed at what his physique might be under the suit, but exactly. The slope of his shoulders. The width of his hips. The... She flushed a little at the mental comparison and shook off the thought.

"You turn such a pretty shade of pink," Kayden said as he knelt on the bed, his hands curling around her thighs and drawing her in close to him. "Whatever is going through that lovely head of yours?"

"You," Mya answered truthfully.

Kayden looked entirely too pleased with himself at the answer, and she rather wished she hadn't given it, but there was nothing to be done about it when the word had already left her lips.

"You are quite a pleasure to regard, yourself," he said, leaning down to brush his lips over the shell of her ear and making her breath hitch as his blew warm over her skin. There was a tension in his voice that said he was trying not to laugh. "I think we make a handsome couple."

Mya hooked a leg around his hip to drag him closer. "Stop admiring yourself and do something useful, would you?"

"As you wish."

In the next moment, he was pressing inside her, groaning against her neck as he filled her with a long, slow thrust. Mya echoed the sound, spine curving and toes curling, arching up into the weight of his body against her own.

He felt familiar. Like her body knew his. Like safety, and warmth, and pleasure burning its way through the core of her. They moved together in an easy rhythm, and Mya let herself go. She met him each time he rocked down, moaned his name without care for who might hear. It didn't matter. All that mattered was Kayden—on top of her, inside her, all around her.

Her nails raked lines down his back, and Kayden hissed pleasure and pain, answering the sting with a bite at the curve of her throat, where it would be hidden by the high collar of her everyday dress.

"Mya," he growled, picking up the pace. "Mya... Damn."

"Yes." Pleasure dragged her eyelids down, but she didn't let them close, kept her gaze fixed on his face. He was looking down at her too, with a hungry intensity in his dark eyes that made the pleasure shared between them somehow stronger. Sharper. "Yes," she said again. "Kayden."

He moved faster still, and harder. Mya could hear the headboard of the bed rocking against the wall, and was once more grateful for the deserted wing they shared. Kayden traced her jawline with his lips, and found her mouth with his.

They rocked like that, wrapped around each other and pressed together at every possible point. It was perfect. Damn perfect. It was amazing. He was amazing, and Mya couldn't think past him and the way he felt. The way they felt together.

He was getting close. She could feel it in the way that his rhythm faltered, knew the way that his breath came in quick pants. His fingers stroked over her waist, her hip. Mya felt the pleasure building at her core, and kissed him hard. Hungry.

They went over the edge together. She cried out, and Kayden muffled a gasp of her name against her shoulder. His hands curled bruisingly tight over the curves of her hips.

Slowly, the hands holding her went lax and fell away. Kayden rolled to the side to avoid putting all his weight down on her, and they lay side by side in the rumpled sheets, both of them panting, and grinning at nothing.

"Useful enough for you?" Kayden asked at last, turning his head so he could watch her profile.

"I would say that I am satisfied with your performance."

"'Satisfied?' Is that all?"

"Mmm." Mya stared up at the ceiling, pretending to consider her answer. "I am not sure. I think it might require a repeat performance, to test the results."

Kayden laughed, and an arm slid beneath her and pulled her to him, her head against his shoulder and her body wrapped around his. "You are a cruel mistress."

"Cruel? Not in the least. I am only demanding. I wish to make sure that you are giving me your best." She tipped her head back to look up at him. "A gentleman must always offer his utmost, after all. "

"This gentleman is going to show you a thing or two in a moment."

Mya sniffed. "I should like to see you try."

"Is that a challenge, my lady?" Kayden asked.

He didn't wait for her answer. As it turned out, he had a thing or two to show her after all.

Chapter 10

The entire household woke late.

At least the three ladies who had partied for the night. Mya couldn't say the same about the maids and staff. Hopefully no one noticed Kayden leaving. He had not left until nearly dawn, sneaking away before anyone entered Mya's room to find him there.

Mya wandered down to breakfast well after noon, to find Eleanora seated at the table and Lottie nowhere to be found. She took a seat across from the other woman, hiding a yawn behind her hand. It had been an amazing night.

"Good morning... or nearly afternoon," Eleanora said, looking up from the book she had been reading and smiling at Mya. "Did you sleep well?"

"Quite well, actually." Mya pulled two pieces of toast from the rack and set them on her plate with an egg and a small pile of orange slices. "I think I tired myself out last night." She glanced around. "Where is Lottie?"

"Lottie is still abed." Eleanora marked her place in the book and set it aside. "She always sleeps particularly late after parties. Tired, as you say." She paused to take a bite of toast. "How was your first ball, now that you have had some time to think on it?"

"I enjoyed it. It was nice to go out, and to meet new people." She wondered if she ought to pry into whatever had happened between Eleanora and Lottie the night before. Would it offend the other woman if she asked? "What of you? Did you enjoy the night?"

Eleanora cut a slice from her sausage, but did not eat it yet. "I did. Though some of the company could have been better."

"Is that what you were upset about last night?" The words were out before Mya had time to stop them.

Eleanora looked up sharply, eyebrows lifted. "I beg your pardon?"

Mya shrank back a little in her seat, wishing she had decided to leave well enough alone. "I saw you and Lottie last night. In the hall. I did not stay to listen, but you looked as though you were unhappy."

"Oh." Eleanora chuckled. "That. I thought you were referring to the ballroom. I would hate to have given our gracious hosts the impression that I did not thoroughly adore their lovely party."

There was an edge to the words that Mya took to mean Eleanora had not thoroughly adored the ball at all.

"We were discussing Mrs. Auteberry's obvious attempt at a slight. Which I could have taken in better grace, I admit."

"A slight?"

"You were there, I think, when she introduced me to that English bloke. She knew quite well I would have no interest in dancing with the man. I suppose it is her way of taking some small revenge for my dislike of her, which she seems to have at last picked up on."

"Is it because he's English?"

Eleanora took a deep breath, and a bite of sausage. When she had finished chewing, she nodded. "I am afraid I am not particularly fond of them, after everything they put this country through. Though please take care not to go around repeating that. There are those who would do more than simply take offense at my attitude."

"I am sorry," Mya said, surprised Eleanora would take a dislike of someone simply because of where they were from. It didn't seem like her. "I don't know much of the history, and did not mean to start an unpleasant breakfast discussion."

"Not at all." Eleanora smiled at her. "As you say, you did not know. It is hardly your fault that you do not know the country's history when you cannot even remember your own." She fell silent then.

Mya wondered if she was going to say anything more. She poured herself a cup of tea, and considered speaking up to change the subject before the silence between them became awkward.

"My family," Eleanora said finally, "has never been terribly fond of the English. We fought against them more than once, and paid the price for that too. After the last rebellion, the English outlawed the kilt and the tartan. That act has since been repealed, and in recent years Queen Victoria's interest in our clothes has made them not only acceptable, but desirable. Yet those English who flock to flaunt their new fashion do not understand that those things were taken from us. That we have only just begun wearing them again. They have no concept of the Highlands, nor of our way of life. And, in truth, it angers me to see it."

"It seems a reasonable complaint to me," Mya said, between bites of egg.

"Of course it does. You are Scottish, whatever forgotten details your history might hold." She tipped her head slightly to the side, regarding Mya thoughtfully. "Though your name is Boyle. That was an opposing clan of ours. So your clan and mine did fight on opposite sides in the Jacobite uprisings. But I will not hold that against you."

She smiled as she said it, and Mya laughed. "I appreciate your generosity, truly."

Lottie appeared in the doorway of the dining room, wearing a dressing gown and still half asleep, her hair loose. She dropped down into a seat next to Eleanora and served herself a pile of cold fish and toast with eggs.

"It is so nice of you to join us, darling," Eleanora said, lips curling up at the corners in a fond, amused smile. "I do hope you slept well?"

"If I had slept any better, I think I would have to be dead," Lottie said. She grinned at Mya. "I think you did not sleep as well as I did. You still look tired. Flushed, but tired all the same."

That, Mya did not explain, was Kayden's fault. He was quite exhausting. She definitely was sure she wasn't ready to share that information with her hosts. At least, not yet.

"It was a very long night," she said instead.

Lottie was too busy eating to answer, and Mya turned to her own food. No one spoke for a short while, all of them thoroughly enjoying their breakfasts. It was surprising how hungry dancing, and other things, could make a person.

One of the maids, entering from the front of the house, broke the quiet.

"Someone here to see you, Miss Boyle," she said, dipping a curtsy. "Do you wish me to tell them you are still breakfasting?"

"Who is it, Anna?" Lottie asked.

"Lord McGregor, miss," the maid answered.

Lottie's eyebrows darted toward her hairline. Eleanora did not seem surprised by the news. She took another bite of toast.

"You have to invite him in, then, Mya."

"I do?"

"Yes," Lottie said emphatically. "I enjoy having something nice to look at in the morning."

Eleanora huffed a quiet laugh at that.

"Anna," Lottie said, turning back to her. "Tell Lord McGregor that he is welcome to join us for breakfast, if he would like."

The maid hurried off, and Eleanora shook her head. "You are not dressed, Lottie," she pointed out, with the air of someone who strongly suspected their good advice was going to be ignored.

"He is not here to see me. He is here to see Mya. Mya is dressed." Lottie took a sip of tea and smiled sweetly at Eleanora. "He will hardly be looking in my direction."

Mya wasn't so sure about that; she couldn't imagine Lottie with her hair loose around her shoulders and her dressing gown sliding down the curve of one would be an easy thing to ignore. She didn't say so. Eleanora's expression said it quite clearly for the both of them.

The maid returned, with Kayden in tow, and he greeted them all with a bow.

"Please," Eleanora said. "Do be seated. You are welcome to anything on the table."

Kayden sat, claiming the seat next to Mya, and took a small bunch of grapes.

"Still suffering the aftereffects of the ball, I see," he said, giving Lottie a pointed look. He, of course, was impeccably dressed already, and didn't look at all as though he had spent most of the night awake.

"I like to indulge myself after such things," Lottie said, shrugging. "It is a lovely thing to have a house of your own in which you can do as you please."

Laughter was her answer to that, and a nod. "Indeed," Kayden said. "I hope I have not disturbed your indulgence, then, with my presence."

"Not at all. Though I might ask what your errand is."

"That," Kayden said, though they had already been told by the maid, "is to call upon Miss Boyle, in the hopes that she might grant me the pleasure of a walk with her this afternoon."

Mya glanced at the other women across the table. Eleanora looked like she was trying not to smile. She gave an encouraging little nod. Lottie, on the other hand, couldn't seem to take her eyes off Kayden.

"I would enjoy that," Mya answered. "Thank you."

Lottie laid a hand over her heart, eyes wide. "An unchaperoned walk with a man you only met a fortnight ago? What *would* your mother say?"

Eleanora hid a laugh in her tea. Mya turned a flat look on Lottie, who just gave her back wide-eyed false innocence.

"Go," she said, laughing. "Enjoy yourselves while you are young."

"I don't think you've had enough sleep," Mya said, shaking her head as she got up from the table. "So I am going to let how odd you are being go for the moment."

Kayden came around the table and offered his arm to Mya. She laid her hand in the crook of his elbow, and let him lead her down the steps from the patio to the garden. They walked together in silence along the paths lined with bluebells, waiting by unspoken mutual agreement until they were outside the earshot of the women at the table to speak.

"I see now," Kayden said finally, "where you have acquired your attitude."

Mya laughed. "I think that would be a reasonable assumption had I lived with Lottie for more than two weeks. My 'attitude' is entirely me, I'm afraid. Though I don't doubt that she has encouraged it."

"Lottie will gleefully encourage any number of things she ought not to."

"You do not like my attitude?" Mya asked, turning to look up at him as they walked.

"I did not say that."

Kayden spun them, abruptly, so that Mya had to take a step back off the path, her back against one of the trees that shaded it, and Kayden's body warm against her own.

"I find I'm rather fond of everything about you," he said, tipping his head down with the words and stealing a languid kiss.

When he stepped back, Mya was reluctant to let him go, her hand lingering against his shoulder until he stepped out of reach and once more gave her his arm.

"You are a flatterer, is what you are," she said, looking at him from under her eyelashes. "I do not know what prize you think you will receive for such a speech, when I have already taken you to bed."

"Maybe I would just like to end up in your bed again."

"Is that so?"

Kayden turned his eyes down to her, and she gave him an expectant look.

"It is so," he said.

"Hmm. I suppose I shall consider it," Mya decided gravely. "Though of course in such circumstances, one must also think of—"

She didn't get to finish. "Mya, look," Kayden cut in, voice hardly louder than a whisper.

Mya turned to follow the direction of his gaze and found the white stag. It stood on the hill, head lifted, and watched them both with wide, dark eyes.

"I wish I had my gun," Kayden said. "Look at that rack."

"What?" Mya spun back to face him, staring. "You can't kill him."

"Why ever not? They're animals. And they make good winter provisions."

"Because you..." She paused, trying to come up with an answer that would satisfy him. "You just cannot," she said finally. "It feels wrong. He's not just a deer. Look at him."

"I am looking at him," Kayden said. "And he looks like a deer to me."

Mya huffed, hooking her arm through Kayden's and bodily pulling him back toward the house.

"Mya." He laughed, letting her do it. "I don't understand. What is the problem?"

She shook her head. "Just trust me on this. You cannot kill him. There's something special about him. He's... You can't do it."

"Fine," he said. "I will not, then." He stopped walking, and Mya was forced to stop with him, turning to look up into his face. "I will not hunt it. I promise." He brushed a lock of hair back from her face, and Mya leaned into the touch with a sigh.

"Thank you," she said, feeling a little silly despite the conviction that she had done the right thing. "I know that I can't really explain it, but it's important."

"If it is important to you, it will be important to me."

She leaned up on her toes and kissed him, and he smiled against her mouth.

"Maybe," she said when she drew back, "I will let you into my bed again after all."

His laughter followed them back to the house.

Chapter 11

"I was thinking about inviting Kayden for supper," Mya said a few days later.

Lottie, who was sitting in front of a mostly empty canvas painted with a few strokes of green, turned around in her chair, eyebrows lifted. "Were you, then?"

He had become something of a fixture in the house since the day after the ball, though he had restricted his visits to proper calling hours. Which was beginning to frustrate Mya a little; she wouldn't have actually minded having him in her bed again, and she was half convinced that he was doing it on purpose to make her come out and say so. She was very near just giving in and letting him have the satisfaction of it.

"It might be nice," she said to Lottie, lifting one shoulder in a shrug and letting it fall. "Unless you have some objection to it?"

"No objection at all." Lottie glanced back at her canvas, head tilted thoughtfully. "Though I might take some care in the matter, if I were you. I have heard rumors that someone else is maneuvering for his affections. Do not take it for granted that you are the only one he is speaking with, if you are not officially courting."

"What?" Mya's fingers curled, crumpling the piece of sewing she was holding. "Who? Why would he not tell me?" She cleared her throat. "I mean, how have you heard? Who is it?"

"I could not say for certain. There are no concrete facts in the matter, though I could make a few guesses. My feeling is he has not told you because he does not consider it particularly important, but there is always a chance that he is playing both ends against the middle and seeing what comes of it. I would not expect it of him, but I have been surprised before."

"So you think he is speaking with me and all the while stringing someone else along?"

"I think that you should ask him what is going on, if you wish to know, and that inviting him to supper is an excellent idea." She stroked the brush over the piece in front of her, gradually shaping a grassy hill. "Though do make sure you give him notice enough. He may want a new suit before he attends."

"A new suit?" Mya laughed a little. "I hardly planned on it being some great formal affair. In fact, the reason I wish to invite him here is so that we do not have to observe all the formalities we might have to in public. I would like to simply talk with him. Actually get to know him beneath the exterior of etiquette that he shows everyone else."

"Then tell him he does not need a new suit," Lottie said, sounding a little as though she had just swallowed back the urge to laugh. "It is your supper. Have it as you wish."

"I will, thank you." She watched for a moment longer as Lottie began dotting flowers across her landscape, then turned and started down the hall toward her own room.

Mya could not have said what it was that so dissatisfied her about the rules. Perhaps if she could remember having learned them young, they would seem a more natural part of life, but she could not, and so they seemed largely superfluous. Meant to control behavior that did not need such tight concern. Or maybe she had just been spoiled by Eleanor and Lottie's lax approach to following the more obscure ones.

She did, however, write him an invitation, rather than simply asking him to his face. It was not, perhaps, a masterpiece of art, but she was rather proud of it, considering =she barely remembered her past and yet she knew how to write.

Kayden's answering note came back quickly, and Mya set about preparing the supper itself.

The day of the supper she had planned dawned clear and bright, and Mya felt as though it was a sign that she was on the right path. Or at least a good omen for the rest of the day. She hummed to herself as she dressed and did her hair, and then went to the kitchen to check on the progress of the meal, which was going exactly as planned. If he *was* seeing anyone else, she thought a little smugly, he wasn't going to be after supper.

Lottie and Eleanora had elected not to attend dinner with her and Kayden, citing at the last minute some engagement elsewhere that Mya did not entirely believe existed. They were likely just giving her space, but she was hardly going to complain about that. Time alone with Kayden was not exactly a chore.

When he arrived, the sun was just beginning to set. Mya was waiting in the sitting room when the maid let him in, and they walked together into the dining room, her hand on his arm.

"You are not wearing a new suit," she commented as they crossed the threshold.

"No," he said. "I was not given time to have one made."

"That was the point of it." Mya smiled. "I am tired of silly rules, and I wished to have you here sooner, rather than later."

"I see, however, that you are wearing a new gown." Kayden's eyes moved slowly over her as she took her seat, and Mya smoothed the blue silk of the skirts back into place with a laugh.

"Yes," she said. "But I did not have it made specifically for this dinner."

"It is spectacular." Kayden sat down, his eyes still on her.

Those lingering looks were exactly the reaction she had wanted. Mya hid her smile with a dip of her head, and wondered if he would manage to drag his eyes away from the décolletage revealed by the low neckline of the dress any time soon. "You are too kind."

He laughed at that, obviously amused by her demure response.

The maid stepped into the room with the first course of the meal, setting a tureen on the table and ladling stew into their bowls.

Kayden took a bite and paused, eyebrows drawing together. "What is this?"

"Rabbit stew," Mya answered, a little uncertain. She ought to have made sure he liked it before she had put it on the menu. What if he hated rabbit, or something?

"It is very good." He paused a moment, as though not sure whether he ought to continue or not. "Did you choose it for any particular reason?"

Mya shook her head. "It just felt... right. I've had it once before and quite enjoyed it. I hoped you would as well."

"I do," Kayden said. "I was just surprised to find it on your table, I think. Though I'm not sure why."

"I have that feeling sometimes. Where you aren't expecting something, and then it happens and you realize that maybe you were expecting it after all. And it feels so..."

"Strangely familiar?"

"And somehow as though it was exactly what should have happened all along."

"Yes," Kayden said. "That is it exactly."

He took another bite of the stew, and she saw that same frown flicker across his face before it was gone again. A look like he was trying to remember something that he couldn't quite grasp.

"So," she said when they had both finished their bowls and were waiting for the next course. "You know that I have no idea who my family is. But I would love to know of yours."

Kayden paused in the middle of setting his bowl to the side. "I am afraid there is not much to talk about."

"You do not have to lay out every moment of your life with them," Mya said, laughing a little. "But I think we have been spending a great deal of time together, and it is likely proper that I at least know something of them. That is all." She smiled. "And, I admit, I would like to know the people who raised a man like you."

She had expected Kayden to laugh too, to ask if that was meant to be a compliment or an insult. But he didn't laugh. He said nothing at all, staring down at the plate of food the maid had just brought out instead of looking at her. Mya frowned.

"Kayden? Did I say something wrong?"

He looked up, then, slowly, like he was reluctant to meet her eyes. "No," he said. "You did not."

"Then why will you not answer my—"

"Why will you not let it alone?" he demanded, cutting her off. "I think I have made it clear that it is not a subject I wish to talk on, and yet you continue to push as though you have any right to know. We have spent how many days together? Three? And before that you treated me as though you could not stand me. So I do not see why you thought it would be proper to ask about them."

Startled by the sudden tirade, Mya straightened up in her seat, glaring across the table at Kayden. "They are hardly national secrets, surely. Is it not expected that one would ask after family? Even with the barest acquaintance, it is a topic that is safe to discuss."

"And yet, I think, if the barest acquaintance asked you to drop the subject, you would do so. Is it only me that you will not respect?"

"With someone I hardly knew, I would not feel shut out," Mya said, trying to drop the discussion back to a more reasonable tone. "I care for you, Kayden. We have been more intimate together than I have ever in my memory been with anyone else. Does it matter that it has only been days?"

Kayden laid his fork down. "That I have been to bed with you does not make you privy to things about my life I do not wish to share," he said, voice cool. "It affords you no special privileges, Miss Boyle."

Mya stood up so quickly she nearly knocked her chair over. "Get out."

He seemed to realize, in that moment, what he had said. His eyes widened.

Mya was not going to let him sit there as though someone else had spoken the words, however. They had quite clearly come out of his mouth. "Out, I said."

"Mya..." He reached across the table for her hand, and she yanked it back.

"If I am not afforded any 'special privileges,' Lord McGregor, then neither are you. Go eat dinner in your own manor. I do not wish to look at your face any longer."

For a moment, she thought he would try to protest further, but he did not say whatever was on the tip of his tongue, only turned and walked out without a word.

Mya sank back into her chair and dropped her face into her hands, wondering how a night that was supposed to be magical had gone so terribly wrong.

Chapter 12

"Mya?"

Eleanora's voice broke into Mya's thoughts, and she looked up from the food she was listlessly poking at with a fork to find both Ella and Lottie standing in the doorway of the dining room, looking at her with surprised concern on their faces.

"What happened?" Lottie demanded.

Mya shrugged, and stabbed at a bite of fish with particular viciousness. "Kayden and I had a disagreement. We fought."

"Over what?" Eleanora's tone was gentle, and she moved as she spoke, coming to sit down at Mya's side. Lottie took the other chair.

"I asked him about his family," Mya said. "How was I to know that it is a capital offense?"

There was a moment of silence, the other two exchanging a glance over Mya's head that she didn't know how to interpret.

"It is not your fault," Lottie said. "You did not know that he does not speak of it. I imagine he thought that you had heard some gossip about that, and thought to coax it out of him."

"If he thinks that I would do that, then perhaps it is better that he's gone," Mya said.

If he would not let her know him, and he did not know her at all, then there was little point in their attempting to continue an intimate relationship. Eleanora laid a hand on her shoulder. "He is a hard man to judge sometimes. There is a bit of a temper there, though I have rarely seen him lose it." Her fingers tightened just a little, comforting her. "Did he shout at you?"

Mya shook her head. "No shouting. Though he was very harsh. He said some things that I would consider rather cruel. Those, at least, he seemed to regret after, though I did not let him remain to apologize. I was not in the mood."

"I am sure he will be back, then." Eleanora glanced at Lottie, then back to Mya. "If he did not have a chance to apologize and he thought himself in the wrong, he will want to make that right. When he does come for that, you ought to at least speak with him."

"Why?" Mya laughed unhappily. "He treated me as though I was attacking him, and came very near to calling me a whore. If he comes and grovels on his knees I might consider forgiving him, but I am not going to let him walk in here with some nonsense about a misunderstanding."

"Nor should you," Lottie cut in. "Ella didn't say you have to forgive him. Just that you ought to at least hear him out. I think that is a reasonable thing to do. Though if you wish to draw it out a little, I am hardly going to stop you." She flashed a smile that faded quickly into a more serious expression. "Only do not let yourself stew in anger too long. It will not help you or hurt him."

"That is not fair." Mya sighed, and dropped her head to lean against Lottie's shoulder. "I am not saying that I will never forgive him, or that I will go about hating him forever. But he was far over the line of proper behavior, and not in a manner that is acceptable."

"We will turn him away, then, if he returns," Eleanora said. "But only for a week."

"I suppose that is time enough," Mya admitted. "Very well."

One week.

She could deal with him then.

Kayden, of course, did not wait a week.

Lottie reported that he was at the door the next day, asking to be let in to speak with Mya. She sent him away, but kept the bouquet he had carried with him, placing it in a vase on the dining room table. Eleanora examined it with some fascination.

"It is a lovely apology," she said that night at dinner. "Though I am sure that, should you choose to actually speak to him, he will accompany it with words as well."

Mya's eyebrows lifted. "The flowers are an apology?"

"Oh, yes," Eleanora said. "Each of the blossoms has a meaning, you see. He has very nearly made a speech with this." She motioned to the heavy purple heads of the hyacinth. "This is sorrow. And apology. The little ones, here, are harebell. They mean humility."

It was a rather nice gesture, Mya had to admit. Sweet, almost. "Do you think I ought to speak to him, then?" she asked.

Lottie tapped a finger thoughtfully against her lower lip, the smile settling there a clear giveaway of her intentions. "No," she said. "I believe you ought to let him worry a short while longer. It might do him some good."

Mya laughed, and despite Eleanor's sigh, decided to take Lottie's advice.

The second day, Kayden returned with a bouquet of little purple and yellow flowers, with petals like velvet. Mya took them from Eleanora and ran her fingers over the softness of the blossoms.

"What do these mean?" she asked quietly.

"They mean you are in his thoughts," Eleanora said.

"I should hope I am," Mya said. "After what happened."

"You are enjoying this a little too much." Lottie chuckled, plucking a grape from the bowl of fruit in front of her.

Mya turned to look at her, eyes wide. "I could not possibly have any idea what you might mean. You are the one who told me I ought to let him be when I asked after yesterday's bouquet. I am only taking the sage advice of someone far more experienced in these matters than I."

Lottie just shook her head. "I invented that look, darling. I am hardly going to fall for it."

"You invented nothing," Eleanora said, looking up from her plate. "I am certain you only stole it from someone else. One of those children always running about and getting in the way and pretending as though they have no idea that they were doing any such thing, most likely."

"You wound me so deeply, my dear."

Mya stifled laughter, and wondered if she ought to speak to Kayden. In truth, though she had made him wait, she did not wish to torment him beyond reason. Only enough that she was certain he meant his apology.

Lottie must have decided the same thing, because the next morning when Kayden came to the door, she let him in without consulting Mya.

"Kayden is here," she said when she walked onto the veranda for breakfast. "I told him he might come in today."

Mya looked up from the toast she was buttering. "Where is he?"

"Waiting in the sitting with a bouquet of geraniums and Love Lies Bleeding." She laughed softly. "I believe he has given up entirely on subtlety and moved on to desperation in the hopes that you will take pity on him."

"I will speak with him," Mya decided. He had waited long enough.

Rising from the table, she found Kayden waiting, as Lottie had said he would be, in the sitting room, staring down at the flowers in his hands.

"Kayden," she said.

His head lifted. "Mya." Relief was light in his voice. "I thought perhaps you would refuse to see me again, even with Lottie to intervene on my behalf."

"I have decided to allow you a chance to speak to me," Mya said, crossing the room and taking a seat on one of the couches. "The bouquets were a lovely touch, I must admit."

"I spent entirely too long deciding what must go in each," Kayden said in return. "I thought if you would not hear me, perhaps you would know what they meant and understand what I was trying to say without words."

"Lottie and Eleanora explained them to me." Mya looked at the cascading red flowers in his hands, sharing space with the pink geraniums. "This one, I think, hardly needs it. Love Lies Bleeding is not a name that is difficult to determine the nature of."

That earned a quiet chuckle. "I thought perhaps if I stopped attempting to be so delicate about it, you might take more notice."

"You have my attention now."

The smile on Kayden's face faded, his expression gone pained, and sincere. "I am sorry, Mya, that I spoke to you in the manner that I did. You did not deserve it, and it was absolutely terrible of me to say such things. I will do whatever you desire to make it up to you."

It was a tempting offer. Mya considered.

"*Whatever* I desire?"

"Whatever you might choose."

"It is a lucky thing for you that you are so handsome," Mya said finally. "Very well. I will accept your apology."

Chapter 13

"There is something I wish to speak with you about," Kayden said later, when they were walking together in the field behind the garden.

Mya turned to look at him, eyebrows raised. "Yes?"

"I will not say that it excused my behavior toward you, but I would appreciate it if you would not press me on the matter of my family. It's a delicate subject for me."

"I hardly pushed," Mya protested. "All I did was ask you the kind of question that anyone might ask, and then ask you why you did not answer it when you brushed me off. Had you said that you simply did not wish to speak of them, instead of going immediately on the defensive, it might have ended differently."

Kayden took a deep breath in and let it out on a rush. "Mya. Please. I'm not accusing you of anything, or yelling at you. I am only asking that you consider my feelings on the matter."

"You are accusing me, though," Mya pointed out, stopping in her tracks and turning completely to look at him. "I'm happy to leave matters of your family to the side, though I do admit that I wonder what you will not say to me, but I hardly acted outside the bounds of propriety."

They began walking again. Kayden said nothing. He was staring straight ahead of them, jaw tight. The warm summer wind rustled in the bushes, filling the air with the faint sighing of leaves. Otherwise, there was only silence. It weighed heavily on Mya's shoulders. This was not the way she had intended their post-apology conversation to go.

"Kayden?" she ventured.

"Yes?" he asked without looking down at her.

"Are you going to refrain from speaking to me at all now? Have I offended you that badly?"

"You have not offended me."

"It's obvious that I have," Mya protested. "You'll not even turn to face me. I told you that I would not bring up your family. What more do you wish me to say?"

"Perhaps, considering that I was gracious enough to offer you an apology for the manner in which I behaved, you would be willing to offer me the same courtesy."

Mya pulled her hand from his arm. "An apology? For what heinous crime have I committed, exactly? How was I to know that you did not speak of your family? I wasn't even told until after you insulted me that you preferred to keep the matter quiet! And frankly," she added, "if the matter of your family is a difficult one, I of all people would understand. I cannot even remember having met mine."

She stalked past him and deeper into the field, toward the shade of a tree that stood near its center. Behind her, she heard the grass hissing against fabric as Kayden followed.

"Mya!" He called after her. "*Mya!*"

She spun around to face him. "*What?*"

"If you want to discuss this, discuss it with me, instead of running away."

"I'm not running away," Mya snapped. "I'm putting some space between us so that I have a moment to think without you breathing down my neck."

She turned away once more and continued onward through the vegetation, pulling her skirts up so they would not snag on it. When she reached the wide trunk of the tree, she leaned back against it, staring up at the cloudy sky through the leaves. She had half expected that Kayden would have gone, returning home rather than continue to deal with her, but when she turned her eyes back to ground level, he was there, standing just outside of arm's reach.

"How can I be breathing down your neck, when I am nowhere near you?" he asked.

"Is it that much of a problem for you? Truly? That I asked about your family at all? In any capacity?"

Kayden sighed. "I admit that much of my anger was based in the thought that you had done it deliberately. And now you act as though I've delivered you some great slight, when all I have done is ask you to acknowledge my own feelings about what happened. I have emotions too, Mya."

"Saint Peter in heaven." Mya laughed disbelievingly, shaking her head. "If you truly wish me to stay so far away from your personal business, perhaps romance is not something we should be engaging in." She turned her face away from him so that he would not see her blinking back the prickling sting of tears. "Do you even desire such a thing with me?"

In a moment, he was at her side, near enough that she could feel the warmth of his body against her own. One of his big hands curled around her chin, turning her back toward him and lifting her face so that their eyes met. "Of course I desire you," he said, voice dropping low in a way that made Mya's heart beat crazily in her chest. "I have wanted you since the moment we ran into each other in that market." He smiled. "I would say sooner, but I am afraid of what it would say about me that I desired an unconscious, bloody woman with an arrow in her shoulder."

"Something hideous, undoubtedly," Mya answered.

Kayden growled, leaning in over her to kiss her, hard and deep. Mya stumbled back a step and came up against the trunk of the tree, one of her arms wrapping around Kayden's shoulders to hold herself up. His hand stroked up her thigh, dragging her skirt with it.

"Are you sure we should be doing this here?" Mya asked when they broke apart, already breathless.

"Who's going to see us?" Kayden asked. "Lottie and Ella know we're out here. They're not going to come looking for us, trust me. Both of them are well aware of what they might find if they choose to come out here. And I am quite sure neither of them has any interest in seeing it." He kissed her again, a brief brush of lips. "The land adjoining is mine, and I am already here. We have the field to ourselves, and I have no interest in waiting long enough to get you inside. Besides, we're less likely to get caught out here. Not so many members of the staff running around."

"Dammit," Mya said. "Shut up."

His laughter vibrated against her skin, and he retaliated by biting down on her shoulder through the fabric of the dress she was still wearing, a bruising pressure just the right side of pain. Mya's fingers curled against his shoulder. Her other hand was pressed palm first to the trunk of the tree, feeling the rough bark against her skin.

"There is no possible way I'm attempting to get all of this nonsense off you," Kayden panted, lifting his head to kiss her jaw and the curve of her ear. "If it's ruined, I'll buy you another."

"Another what?"

"Another whatever. An entirely new wardrobe. I could not care less what the expense is if it means I don't have to waste any time fiddling with all the catches and fasteners and endless layers they insist on strapping you into."

He caught her around the backs of her thighs and lifted her, her body braced between his and the tree that was definitely going to ruin the back of her gown. Mya wrapped her legs around his hips. Kayden didn't even bother taking anything she was wearing off, just pushed her skirts up around her hips and slid his fingers into the opening of her drawers, stroking her.

"So ready for me already, my darling," he groaned. "Fuck."

In the next moment, he had his hand back around her thigh and he was pushing up into her, gravity dragging her down until she could not take him any deeper. Her arms wrapped around his shoulders, and he buried his face against the valley between her breasts as his hips rocked against her own. Mya, unable to let her head fall back against the tree, curved down over him, using his shoulders as leverage. There wasn't much she could do except take it at the pace he gave, gasping with the delicious friction of him filling her to the hilt. The breathless sounds they made mingled with the rustle of the leaves above and the succus of the wind in the grass below.

Overhead, the clouds split at last, and the warm rays of the summer sun spilled down over them, painting Kayden's dark hair with flashes of gold and bronze. Mya felt the friction of the bark against the fabric of her dress, a constant steady vibration running up and down her spine, in perfect counterpoint to the rhythm of Kayden's thrusts.

"Perfect," he panted as he moved. "Mya, you are so utterly perfect."

"Don't talk," she gasped. "Just—" Her cry of pleasure cut off the words. "Just take me."

It seemed that Kayden was more than happy to oblige.

They rose toward the peak of ecstasy together, the rushed gasps for breath tangling together with the sounds of Kayden's groans and Mya's shuddering moans. She felt her body drawing tight, felt the tension in his shoulders wound taut as a strung bow. One more thrust, one more roll of his hips against her, and both of them were falling over the edge, jumbled syllables of each other's names on their tongues.

Kayden's knees gave out, and he slid them both slowly down to kneel in the grass, her skirts tumbled around them. Mya let her head fall back against the tree, eyes rolled upward, and tried to remember what it was to breathe as her racing heart slowed its frantic beat.

"I..." He trailed off, like he didn't know what to say, his voice muffled by her body. He still had his face between her breasts, breathing in the scent of her as he recovered.

Mya reached down and trailed her fingers through his hair. She didn't have words either. Silence settled over them, but it was not awkward. They were both warmly content, basking in the afterglow of pleasure. Mya had forgotten their fight entirely, as it seemed Kayden had.

She wasn't even sure she remembered how to be angry, after that. The thought made her smile. She was going to have to be careful around him, or she was never going to be able to stay mad. Spectacular sex was a relationship hazard.

"You are dangerous," she said.

"Mmm."

He didn't even lift his head. Apparently he was in the process of falling asleep right there on the grass. Mya chuckled softly. It seemed some things were a guarantee after all.

Chapter 14

The morning had moved toward noon by the time Mya returned to the house. Together, they decided it would be best if Kayden returned to his own manor, alleviating suspicions, though Mya was not sure exactly who they were trying to hide their activities from, considering that Ella and Lottie, as Kayden had said, almost certainly knew what they had been up to. And if they didn't already, they were going to now. The back of her dress was a wreck.

Mya reached behind herself again, feeling the fabric that had practically shredded between the tree trunk and the steel bones of the corset. Lottie was almost certainly going to laugh at her. She would have to keep the whole thing away from the maids, who were probably as aware of what was going on as the other inhabitants of the house. Or more aware, likely. That didn't mean that Mya wanted them seeing firsthand the obvious damage or speculating about what had caused it.

Attempting to make it back into the house without getting caught was, unfortunately, easier said than done. Mostly because Lottie and Ella were waiting in her room, sitting together on the bed. Mya felt her cheeks flushed, and knew she must be scarlet all the way down to the neck of her gown.

"Oh," she said, stopping in her tracks with her hand still curled around the edge of the open French door. "I didn't expect the two of you to be here... In here, rather... This specific room, I meant."

The corner of Lottie's mouth twitched upward, though she managed not to smile outright. Eleanora hid a laugh behind her hand in a neatly executed cough.

"We thought we would wait here and make sure that you hadn't fallen in a hole or some such thing out in the fields," Lottie said, obviously struggling to keep a straight face. "You were gone quite some time, after all."

"I do hope you are well?" Eleanora added.

If they were any more pleased with the gossip they had picked up, Mya thought, the both of them would be giggling like children. She gave them a disapproving look. "I am just fine. Thank you."

"And Kayden?" Lottie asked, pretending to look behind Mya, as if expecting Kayden to appear any moment. "He made it home safely, I assume?"

"I'm sure he did."

Mya edged around the room, toward the closet, hoping to slip into the dressing room and change there, without them seeing the damage to the back of her dress. She had, of course, no such luck.

"Grass stains on the back?" Lottie asked, with the air of someone who had experienced just that particular trouble.

"What?" Mya blurted. "No! There aren't any grass stains. What on earth would give you that idea?"

"Perhaps," Eleanora suggested, "the fact that you are attempting to move all the way around the room while still facing us. And the babbling."

"Also the blushing," Lottie said. "You went an even brighter red just now when I asked about grass stains."

Mya sighed. There was going to be no getting past them, it seemed. "There are no grass stains," she said again.

The other two women looked at her expectantly.

Slowly, shaking her head, Mya turned around...and waited.

There was a moment of silence. Mya wasn't sure whether they were startled, or appalled. When she glanced back over her shoulder, they were both staring at the back of the dress.

Lottie broke the silence first, clapping her hands delightedly together. "How did...? No," she said, laughter filling up the words. "Those are, admittedly, not grass stains. I think those are better than grass stains. What do you think, dear?"

Eleanora bit her lip, her eyes dancing with laughter. "Certainly a unique sort of wear and tear."

"It is actually rather impressive, I think," Lottie said. "I have never been accused of being traditional in my... adventures, but I have never done such things... up against a tree?" She looked up at Mya, head tipped to the side in question. "Did you enjoy it?"

Mya groaned softly, covering her face with her hands, and pretended that neither of them existed.

A moment later, there was movement, and then Lottie was beside her, laying a hand over her shoulder. "Mya?"

"Mmm?"

"You know that we do not mean to actually shame you? It is only the sort of teasing shared between friends. There is no judgment here."

"We are hardly the people to hold your desires against you," Eleanora said, still sitting on the bed if the direction her voice came from was anything to go on.

Reluctantly, Mya lifted her head, regarding Lottie through her fingers. "There is no need to harp on it so," she said.

"We only harp on it because it is terribly exciting." Lottie grinned at her. "We have not had anything so scandalous happen here in quite some time. I am afraid that we are both living vicariously through you. It is not fair, but such is life."

At that, Mya laughed. It was rather impossible not to. "Sometimes," she said, "I wonder why I am friends with you."

"Because I am a lovely person," Lottie answered without pause for thought. "And because we are allowing you to live in our house without any sort of rent, which is rather the sort of thing that friends do."

That was, in fact, true. "I suppose that is sufficiently balanced reasoning."

"I presume, then, that you are finished with avoiding Lord McGregor?" Lottie dropped back onto the edge of the bed and looked up at Mya. "Or have you found some new reason to shun him?"

"No," Mya said, shaking her head. "I have not found any reason to shun him. We have dealt with the disagreement, and decided to continue on as we were."

"I am glad to hear it." Lottie smiled. "He was a bit of a mess when you would not let him in to apologize. I am not sure he is quite prepared to be shut out so."

Then he should not have spoken so nastily to her. But Mya didn't say that. They had, as she said, dealt with the disagreement, and she was not going to drag it all out again when her hosts seemed more than ready to move past the issue entirely. In truth, Mya herself was rather ready to be done with it as well.

"Wait! Did you say continue on as before?" Lottie grinned wickedly, even more pleased when Mya didn't answer.

"Would you like some help getting yourself out of the dress?" Eleanora asked, changing the subject without being too jarring about it. "Since waking from your wound, it appears you have not had so much practice with it." She smiled tenderly. "You remember how to do many things, but some seem new to you, like you've never done them before. It makes me wonder..." She waved her hand. "Never mind. Why don't I help you?"

Mya looked down at the dress she was still wearing. "Is there any point in bothering to preserve it?" she asked. "Or is the back too shredded for a tailor to do much about the damage?"

"The skirt could perhaps be salvaged," Eleanora said after a moment. "We can cut it from the gown entirely and hem it into a separate piece. The bodice, I think, is beyond rescue. As for the corset, we will have to see what that looks like beneath, but I think it will still serve its purpose, even if it is a little less pretty than it had been."

"You should perhaps consider not using trees as support in such situations," Lottie said. "In future. If you wish to avoid doing any further damage to your wardrobe."

"Yes," Mya said, laughing. "Thank you. I should never have thought of such an idea on my own."

"That is what I am here for," Lottie agreed.

Mya ducked into the dressing room and began stripping off the ruined dress. The mirror told her that the corset was not too badly damaged. A little rent in the fabric here and there, but that hardly mattered. She pulled on a long skirt and a blouse, and attempted to put her hair back in some semblance of order.

"I do have some news that is relevant to your interests, I believe," Lottie said from the main room, voice pitched to carry.

"And what is that?" Mya asked, leaning into the mirror.

"It appears that the Auteberrys have their sights set on Lord McGregor as a suitor for their daughter. Seems they think he is quite the match for her."

Deciding that there was nothing else to be done with her hair, Mya pinned a last loose lock back and stepped back out of the dressing room. "The Auteberrys? Does Kayden have any interest in Blanche, do you think?"

"Why would you even ask?" Lottie stared at her, shaking her head.

"Kayden has eyes for no one but you, dear," Eleanora said kindly.

"I do not think he would see her naked and dancing the tarantella in front of him if you were in the room," Lottie said. "And in fact I do not put much stock in the rumors. Kayden has never shown much interest in English women. I do not know what would make the Auteberrys think that he might look any differently on their daughter."

"Everyone believes people will look differently on their daughter," Eleanora said. "But I do not believe that you need be worried, Mya. Truly, Kayden is not going to look for another. He is quite smitten. You have no cause for alarm."

"I am not alarmed," Mya said defensively. "I am the one he has been walking with this last week, and the one to whom he brought flowers." She wondered if she was trying to convince them, or herself.

Either way, it settled some of her concern to know that Kayden was not and never would be interested in Blanche Auteberry. Jealousy was hardly a rational emotion, after all. But there were some paths of logic that even it could follow.

She was the one Kayden had gone to his knees for, and the one he could not keep his hands from. If young Miss Auteberry had ever intended to be competition for his affections, she had lost the fight before it even began.

Unless of course, she was a distraction, and Kayden McGregor was looking for someone with a title or money to keep his Lordship intact.

No. Mya shook her head. Kayden only had eyes for her. And she, for him.

Chapter 15

Though Mya had not, to her knowledge, been up into the hills beyond the city, she could have sworn she knew them somehow. Knew the way the air of them would feel against her skin, and the view down to Inverness, curled against the shore where Beauly Firth met Moray.

The heather was all in bloom, and the earthy, sweet scent of it hung on the air, mingling with the hum of the bees in the blossoms. Mya closed her eyes and breathed in the fresh summer morning, luxuriating in the breeze that brushed her cheek and curled around her shoulders. Just ahead, Kayden's mount carried a picnic basket full to the brim with luncheon supplies, courtesy of Lottie and Eleanora. Mya gave her horse a little nudge, and the mare trotted forward to walk side by side with Kayden's gelding.

"Thank you," Mya said, just loud enough to be heard.

Kayden turned to look at her. "For what?"

"For today. It is so lovely here."

He smiled, the promise of something up ahead in his eyes. "You haven't even seen the best of it yet. We will get there."

"I am holding you to that," Mya said.

For a time, they rode together in silence, simply enjoying the sunlight that made it down through the clouds, and the sounds of the world around them. It was a breezy day, the gusts of wind that whirled through the heather keeping the midges away.

"There is something I wish to tell you," Kayden said finally.

Ahead of them, a crofter's hut was nestled in a hollow, smoke rising from the chimney. Lunch, perhaps, Mya thought. The scent of wood smoke drifted down to overwhelm the heather for a moment before the wind blew it away. Mya shivered, though it was not cold. The scent had been so shockingly familiar. For a moment she had felt the warmth of a fire against her skin, heard the murmur of a voice in her ear. But it was gone as quickly as it came.

"Mya?" Kayden prompted.

She shook her head, willing the odd feeling away, and smiled at him. "Yes?"

"I would like to tell you something, if you wish to listen."

"Of course." Mya watched him watch the landscape ahead, his expression thoughtful.

"The reason I do not talk about my family," he said finally, "is that I don't know them."

Mya stared at him. She almost opened her mouth to ask why in the world he had been such an arse about it when she asked, then, when he knew that she didn't know who her family was either. She was hardly going to judge him for being in the same circumstance.

But he was opening up to her, at last, and she didn't want to ruin it. She didn't ask.

"When you say you don't know them..."

He sighed. "I mean that I have never, to my knowledge, met them. When I arrived here, I was taken in by a man who had room, and generosity enough to give aid to strangers without expecting anything in return. Much like what Lottie and Eleanora have done for you. But he was an older man, and as his health declined, I became more and more involved in looking out for him. Eventually I was the person doing most of the caretaking."

His voice caught, briefly. Mya would not have heard it if she had not been listening so intently.

"So when he... passed on, he left his lands and money to me. He had no family any longer. No heirs. Without him, I would be nowhere and nothing."

"And now you are a lord," Mya finished.

Kayden laughed. "Yes. Indeed. Though sometimes I think that particular bit of good fortune is more trouble than it's worth."

"Is McGregor his name, then?" Mya asked.

"No." Kayden shook his head. "It's mine. I did not wish to trade it. Even though I can't remember my family, I would like to keep that connection to them. I am sure you understand."

Yes, Mya understood. She too knew exactly what it was to have lost a family you couldn't even mourn because you didn't know who they were. What they had been like. Whether you shared anything with them beyond a name.

"Would you trade it?" Mya asked.

Kayden's eyebrows lifted. "Trade what?"

"The life that you've had, for the one you might have had with your family? The old man who took you in. Do you think you would forget ever having known him, if you could know the family you were born to, or would you rather keep what you have than go for the unknown?"

Kayden sighed, frowning down at the reins in his hands. "That is not an easy question to answer."

"No," Mya said. "That's why I asked it. I want to know what you would choose."

"I think it's a bit of a moot question anyway, isn't it? It's hardly as though one of the fair folk is going to show up and ask us whether we would make the trade or no."

"Well, no. But it's still an interesting question. One most people don't have to ask themselves." She shrugged, and nudged her horse forward. "I still haven't been able to answer it, myself."

"Haven't you?" Kayden, his horse keeping pace with her own still, looked over at her. "I thought perhaps you'd come up with one and were waiting to see if I gave the same answer."

Mya laughed. "No. I'm not sure that it's a question anyone actually can answer. On the one hand, you have your family. The people who are meant to mean everything to you. But they mean nothing, because as far as you are aware, you have never met them. You know nothing of them, whether they were good or bad, clever or stupid, kind or not. On the other, you have the people you know, who have taken you in. And though they might still be veritable strangers, you know that they are good, and clever, and kind. That they care for you."

She looked up at the clouds moving across the sky, here and there leaving patches of blue visible for a moment or two before hiding them again. Ahead of them, something rustled through the heather and away, avoiding the horses' feet.

"Is it better to take the known quantity, with which you are happy, or the unknown, with which you might be happier, but you also might lose what happiness you had?"

Was it better, she wondered, to have a family? Or to have Ella and Lottie and Kayden? And in that moment she knew. If she had ever had to choose, if it ever came to that, she would choose the man beside her. Every time.

"I don't believe I'm quite ready for such questions," Kayden said finally. "You have bested me with that one."

"It was not meant to be a contest, you know," Mya said, letting a little laughter slide into her voice.

"All the same, I am not clever enough for such things," Kayden answered, turning a smile on her. "You will have to refrain from them, I think, or I may damage myself trying to work it out."

That was something she rather doubted, but Mya just laughed and let him be. She had no more such questions anyway.

How old had he been, Mya wondered, when he had been taken in by the man who gave him his title? Young, surely, if he had forgotten his family entirely. Or had he skipped some intermediate step? A family who had been meant to take care of him but had used him as free labor? The workhouse? For a moment, she played with the idea that perhaps that was not his story at all. That maybe his was similar to her own and that he had not been young when he lost his family, only lost the memory of them as well.

But that was something of a stretch, wasn't it? Two people in the same circle who had woken one day with no memory of where they had come from and only little idea of who they were. For such a thing to happen would be entirely too much coincidence. Mya shook the idea away.

"Kayden?"

"Yes?"

"When were—?"

She didn't have the chance to finish the question before he was kicking his horse into a canter. Mya sighed and followed. He might have given her some warning, at least.

Over the crest of the ridge, they came upon a group of little hills, all running down into a dip in the landscape where water had pooled, blue and clean and circled with reeds. Down by the edge of the pond, stones stuck up out of the water, green with moss.

"This is the place that I mentioned," Kayden said, sliding off his horse and grinning at her as he turned a slow circle with arms stretched out wide to indicate the area. "Isn't it lovely?"

"It is."

Mya thought of asking the question again, and of getting a genuine answer, but Kayden was already pulling the picnic supplies from their place and spreading out a blanket on the heather in view of the pond. He looked so pleased that Mya could not bring herself to drag up the uncomfortable subject of his family yet again. There would be time later to discuss it. For the moment, she would simply enjoy his company.

They took the bridles from the horses to let them graze, and set out the picnic. There were cold meats and fish, cheese and fruit and bread. She also happened to know that Lottie had sent leftover chocolate tart. But Kayden did not. That was a surprise.

He passed her a plate, and she scooped bits of her favorite dishes onto it, then sat back to eat.

There was something about eating out in the open that made one's appetite greater, Mya thought as she took a bite of smoked fish from Sunday's dinner. Perhaps it was all the fresh air. Or the riding. But the food tasted better than it ever had.

"My compliments to the cooks," Kayden said, pausing for the first time between bites. "I must admit, I have missed the spreads that Lottie used to put out for parties. This makes up for it, somewhat." He smiled. "And also makes me regret even more that I did not actually finish dinner with you the other night."

For an instant, Mya felt anger. He was going to make light of that after all the trouble it had caused? All the hurt? But he was not making light of the incident, she realized in the next breath. He was making a joke at his own expense.

"You missed dessert," Mya said. "Which is a great pity. I assure you that it would have been an experience to remember."

"And now you rub it in my face." Kayden laughed. "How very uncharitable of you, Miss Boyle."

"Not a bit." Mya smiled sweetly at him. "If I was going to rub it in your face, I would tell you exactly what ingredients went into it, and how perfectly the flavors of the fruit mixed with the sweet cream and the bitterness of the chocolate."

"Now you are just being cruel."

"Yes," Mya agreed. "Now I am being cruel."

Kayden set his plate very carefully down, and in the next instant had curled his palm around the back of her neck and dragged her forward into a kiss. Mya very nearly dropped the plate she was still holding, and had to fumble to set it aside so that she could lean forward and return the kiss as hungrily as he had given it.

"Was that a punishment?" Mya laughed when he released her. "Or an incentive to do it again?"

"Neither." Kayden picked up his plate again, smoothing his hair back into place with a quick slide of his palm. He looked as though he had never moved from the spot where he sat. "It was you, with that little smirk on your face. I could not resist."

"I will have to wear it more often, then."

They both fell silent, after that, finishing up their meals and packing up the picnic. Mya then got up and dug into her own saddlebags to pull out the wrapped tart, carrying it back to the blanket. Kayden was lying on his back, staring up at the clouds.

"I thought," Mya said, "that you might like some dessert."

He sat up so quickly he nearly ran his face into the tart she was holding out, and Mya had to snatch it back before it was ruined.

"I wasn't informed that you have a sweet addiction." She laughed.

"Not sweets. Only that chocolate tart Lottie's cook makes."

"This chocolate tart?" Mya teased, holding it out to him once more.

Kayden made a hungry sort of sound that went straight down Mya's spine to her core, and suddenly she was less interested in food and more interested in getting him to make that noise again. He reached out, and she slapped his hand back.

"Wait. Good heavens. Do you desert your manners entirely in the presence of chocolate?"

"Woman," Kayden growled. "If you do not share some of that, I swear I will not be responsible for what happens next."

Mya was laughing too hard to keep the tart out of his reach any longer, and Kayden pulled it from her hands and set it down on the blanket, rummaging in the basket for a knife to slice it with. He cut it so quickly she was a little afraid he was going to lose a finger in the process, but he managed to avoid any carnage and served up two slices, diving immediately into his with a moan that was positively sexual. It was a wonder, Mya thought, that he'd lasted long enough to not just dig into it with his hands.

"It is a lucky thing I didn't feed that to you in public," she said, shaking her head. "You would have traumatized someone."

Kayden didn't answer. He was too busy eating. Laughing once more, Mya gave up and started on her own dessert at a rather more reasonable pace. Kayden too had slowed, at least, and was no longer imitating some form of desperate beast. Now he was savoring each bite, eyes rolling frequently upward, with the accompaniment of the occasional groan of pleasure, and if he did not stop making those sounds Mya was going to combust.

Taking a leaf out of Kayden's book, she moaned over her own bite of tart. Kayden's hand stilled on his fork. Mya, pretending she did not see the pause, continued on, this time making a sound that she knew he would remember quite well from a few nights before. When he looked up at her, she was licking the last trace of chocolate from her fork with the tip of her tongue.

Their eyes met. Mya smiled slowly.

"You," Kayden growled as he set his half-finished dessert unceremoniously aside, "are unbelievable."

"Hardly," Mya said, taking another bite of tart. "I am simply—"

He didn't give her time to finish her answer before his mouth claimed hers. Mya was more than happy to play along.

Chapter 16

"Do you know what the best thing about this place is?" Kayden asked, Mya's jacket entirely unbuttoned and his mouth on her neck.

"Hhm?" Mya gasped. "Wh-What is it?"

"That no one is going to come out here and find us, which means that I can take my time with you."

As though to prove his point, he tugged her up into a sitting position. She helped him pull the jacket off, and they tossed it aside. He threw his own coat to join it. Kayden leaned in again to kiss her, his fingers already on the buttons of her blouse.

"You're sure?" she asked. "No one?"

"Quite sure," Kayden said.

Mya wasn't entirely certain what kind of proof he had for the claim he was making, but she decided that she was just going to give in and go with it. If someone stumbled upon them, someone did. She wasn't sure that she would even care in a few more minutes if the entire population of Inverness came trooping up the rise and watched them.

"Up," Kayden said. "Come on."

He drew her to her feet, and Mya reached for his clothing as he finished stripping her out of the thankfully simple riding skirt. The corset, of course, would still take a little doing.

Mya tugged at the collar of his shirt, and Kayden let his arms drop for a moment so she could slide it off of him. His undershirt and her petticoat followed.

Pants, corset, chemise, bloomers... Eventually everything was laid aside on an unoccupied corner of the blanket and they were both bare in the warm sunlight. Kayden lowered Mya back, following her down, and she looked up into dark eyes gone even darker with want. He leaned toward her, and his lips brushed hers.

When he drew back, Mya tried to follow, reaching for him, but Kayden shook his head. "No," he said, voice gone deeper, rougher at its edges. "Stay. For me?"

Mya nodded, sinking back to the blanket. If Kayden wished her to stay, she would stay.

At the edges of her vision, she saw him reach for something, dragging it across to his side. Mya's eyes narrowed. She was sure she knew exactly what that was going to be.

True to her expectations, Kayden held out a fork with a bite of tart on it. "Here," he said. "Eat."

"Did you get me naked just so you could feed me chocolate?" Mya asked, laughing. She leaned up and took the bite anyway. It was really good, melting over her tongue with just a hint of sharp salt to cut the sweetness.

"No," Kayden said. He grinned down at her, and she felt his finger stroke a line along the valley between her breasts. "I got you naked so that I can lick chocolate off your body."

Before she had time to reply, he had dipped his head down and followed the line his finger drew with the tip of his tongue. Mya moaned.

"I did not think it was possible for this to get more delicious," Kayden said when he had raised his head again. "But I believe I just found the secret."

His fingers dipped into the tart again, and then he was rubbing them over her nipples, already peaked tight from anticipation and that touch, drawing curling lines across her breasts. Mya bit her lip, her fingers sliding into his hair.

Kayden lowered his mouth to her chest.

Her hand constricted in his hair as soon as his lips met her skin, her back arching, and his name fell from her lips. The sensations he created had Mya teetering between wanting this sweet torture to end and never wanting it to stop. His sinfully wicked tongue lapped up the chocolate and each time it passed over her nipple her other hand tightened in the blanket beneath them. By the time he had licked the last of the chocolate away, Mya's grip was so tight she was sure that the wool would rip beneath her fingers.

"Oh, heavens, Kayden." Her voice was thick with want. "Please, darling."

"I do not think I am quite finished yet," Kayden said.

He dragged a line of chocolate down the center of her body to just above the place she wanted him most, and then followed it slowly, so slowly, with his tongue. Mya swore at him, writhing under the hands that held her hips in place, but he would not let her go, would not move faster than the tortuously slow slide that was driving her mad with need.

"Kayden," she said again. "Kayden. *Kayden.*"

His eyes lifted to her face, and he must have been satisfied at what he found there, because he moved faster, suddenly, teeth scraping gently against her skin between flicks of his tongue.

Mya sobbed his name.

He didn't bother with the chocolate after that, just buried his face between her thighs and licked her until she was bucking against his hands, body undulating and both hands fisted in the blanket. She was close. She was so close, and he knew it. Must have known it.

Kayden pulled away. Mya forced her hazy eyes open and found him sitting back on his knees between her legs, looking down at her.

"What are you doing?" she demanded. "Don't stop, Kayden. Please. Please. I need—"

He caught her around the hips and flipped her abruptly over onto her hands and knees, dragging her back against him and filling her with his length in one smooth thrust.

Mya cried out at the unexpected pleasure, rocking into the stretch of it.

"You're so beautiful," Kayden was saying, leaning down over her to drop kisses along her spine. "I can't get enough of you, Mya. Don't know how I ever lived without you before this."

Mya shuddered with pleasure and desire, arching back to meet his thrusts. Neither of them were going to last very long. She was already on the edge. Kayden's teeth closed over the nape of her neck, biting down just hard enough to sting, and that was it. Pleasure shocked through her, dancing along her spine, and Mya dropped forward onto her forearms as her elbows gave out.

Kayden didn't stop. He just kept going, moving in her, his rhythm hard and fast. Mya groaned, nails catching in the wool of the blanket when her fingers curled and let his hands on her hips move her to match his pace.

"Fuck. Mya." His voice had gone tight.

She was already rising on a new tide of pleasure, carried toward the peak of it. His hands tightened on her hips. His hips moved faster against hers. He groaned his release against her neck. In nearly the same instant, Mya followed him over the edge with a gasp.

Both of them panted, Kayden with his forehead resting between her shoulder blades, and Mya with her cheek turned against her forearm. Kayden slid carefully back and gathered her into his arms, laying them both down on the blanket with her back to his chest and his arm around her waist.

"What do you think?" he asked, and she could feel the rumble of the words in his body pressed against her own.

"I think you have far too strong a fondness for chocolate tart," Mya answered, snuggling contentedly deeper into his embrace.

Kayden laughed.

When they at last dragged themselves up from the blanket, the day had moved well into the afternoon, and the remains of the chocolate tart had completely melted. Kayden stood looking at it ruefully as Mya started the process of getting the layers of her clothes back on.

"Next time," he said. "We're not letting any of the chocolate tart go to waste." He stepped around her back to help her tighten up her corset. "And we're also going swimming."

"Who says you get to decide everything that we do?" Mya asked, trying not to sway too much into the tug of his hands on the stays.

There was a moment of silence behind her. "If you do not like it, Mya, we can do something else. I did not mean to make you feel as though I am always telling you what to do, or demanding that we do something you would rather not."

Mya turned and lifted her hand to his cheek, stroking the line of his jaw where it was a little rough with stubble. "I don't feel that way. I was only teasing you, dearest."

Kayden smiled. "Well, good then. I am not sure if we could continue this relationship if you did not like chocolate tart."

Mya just laughed, shaking her head as she gathered up the rest of her things and settled her riding hat back on the mess her hair had become. "Thankfully, you will never have to find out. I am just as fond of chocolate tart as the next person."

"On second thought," Kayden said thoughtfully, "maybe I should find someone who *doesn't* like it. Then I don't have to worry about them stealing it from me."

"You have far too much stake in chocolate tarts. Especially ones that aren't even in existence yet. Hypothetical chocolate tarts."

"Chocolate tarts are important."

"Get dressed and get on your horse," Mya answered, shaking her head.

Looking entirely too amused with himself, Kayden did as she said, and they rode back down toward Inverness in companionable silence. Mya's thoughts were moving ahead, toward the next time they would be together. Kayden seemed to be still mourning the loss of half a chocolate tart.

They were nearly back to the firth that cut between them and Inverness when they came down a little gully and onto the flat top of a rise that looked down at the water and the city beyond. There was a house there. It was ancient, the walls crumbled down to their foundations and the roof long since gone. Mya could see a little patch of what had, perhaps, been a garden long ago, though it had since gone wild. She slowed her horse.

"Mya?" Kayden looked up, a question in his expression. "What are we doing here?"

"I'm not sure," Mya said, pulling her mount to a halt entirely and sliding from the mare's back.

There was something about the place that...called to her. It felt like something she had done before, standing on that particular rise and looking down at the city. When she turned toward the hills rising behind the ruins of the house, she half-expected to see a stag standing there, his head lifted high and his pale coat turned gold with the afternoon sunlight.

But there was nothing.

"Mya, I am not sure this isn't someone's property."

"If it is," Mya pointed out, gesturing to the overgrown clearing and tumbledown house, "it isn't a property they care for very much."

She turned away from him and made her way through the grass until she was standing in front of the broken, moss-covered foundation. There was nothing to see, of course. No utensils or furniture left behind, the old house gone. Mya blinked back tears that were suddenly welling in her eyes, not sure why they had started.

In a moment, Kayden was beside her, one strong arm around her shoulders and drawing her back away from the building.

"Mya? Darling? Talk to me. What is wrong?"

Mya shook her head. "I don't know," she admitted softly. "I just felt... I feel like there's something here that I remember, but I don't know how I could when it's so obviously been falling down for years. Or decades. Or centuries. Who knows?" She turned to lay her head against his shoulder, shutting out the world beyond him. "It's just a little sad. To see a place that probably held a family be reduced to rubble. People must have been happy here, once, and now they're not."

Kayden held her closer. "This place served its purpose," he said, gently. "It has done what it is meant to do. That it is crumbling, that doesn't mean that memories of what it was go away. They're still here, beloved. They will always be here."

"That's beautiful," Mya said, sniffing a little. "Thank you."

"You are welcome, my dear."

Together, they got back on their horses and rode on toward Inverness, leaving the ramshackle remains of the little house to nature and taking their memories with them.

Chapter 17

"Where are you off to this afternoon?"

Mya, who had been on her way out the door, startled at the unexpected voice behind her and turned to find Lottie sitting on one of the benches that lined the back wall of the veranda, with a book in her hand.

"I am going to see Kayden," she answered.

Lottie's eyebrows lifted. "Things must be going well between the two of you, then. I am glad to hear it."

"They're going well," Mya said with a smile.

Since the day they had ridden up into the hills, things had been going perfectly, in fact. In the last two weeks, she and Kayden had spent most afternoons walking in the fields together, and he had taken her to the theater in Inverness only three nights before. Things, she thought, were going to be heading in a rather more official direction soon.

The visit to Kayden's home was a surprise. She had not been there before; Kayden had always come to see her, or they had met at the boundaries of the two properties to walk together. Mya had seen the home once, from some distance. It was a graceful building, with trees lining the drive, and horses running in paddocks that adjoined the stables. But this was the first time that she would be setting foot in his home.

"I should be back in time for supper," she said as she paused to pull on her gloves. "If I am not, though, there's no need for you to worry."

Lottie laughed. "Mya, darling, I never expect you back in time for supper when you are with Kayden."

Mya blushed at the implication in the words, but she didn't have much of a defense to offer. They didn't always have sex, but whenever she and Kayden were together, they couldn't seem to bring themselves to part. More than once they had simply sat in the shade of a tree and talked, or remained silently side by side in contented quiet. It was a rare thing, that ability to simply sit in quiet with someone and yet feel as though the two of you were connected in that silence. As though you did not even have to speak to be intimate.

Mya could not imagine being happier with anyone else.

She was humming to herself as she walked across the back fields, carrying a wrapped chocolate tart, which she had made just for him to keep in his icebox, where it most definitely wouldn't melt. It was a bit of a walk, but she hardly minded. The weather was lovely, and Mya had always enjoyed walking. There was something about it that made her feel just a little more alive. Connected to the wider world around her.

Up ahead, the shape of Kayden's manor began to reveal itself. There was, Mya saw, a coach in front of the door, which she hadn't expected. It ought to have occurred to her that Kayden might have guests, but she had made the decision to come see him on impulse. He had been busy with work the last three days, and after becoming accustomed to seeing him so frequently, the absence was disappointing.

As she approached the drive, Mya paused to make certain that the hem of her skirt wasn't terribly muddy, and readjusted her hat. Not that Kayden particularly cared whether her hat was on perfectly straight, as he had demonstrated more than once, but she was still making a social call, and Eleanora had taught her the rules of such things well.

When she knocked on the door, it was opened by a uniformed servant, who bowed, and invited her in to wait. Mya, of course, could not quite bring herself to sit politely in the receiving room while the butler went to search the home. Feeling a little mischievous, she got up and crept down the hall, still holding the chocolate tart.

She didn't know whether or not she actually expected to find Kayden. It was likely that he was in his office working, or that he was even out on business. The visitor with the coach might have been with him, holed up in a meeting somewhere. Perhaps, Mya thought, she ought to have waited after all, or sent ahead about calling. There were rules about cards and letting your intentions be known and all those sorts of things. It might have saved her some trouble to have followed them. Kayden was supposed to meet with her again on Sunday anyway; it wasn't really such a long wait. What if he was frustrated that she had showed up while he was busy?

The sound of voices quietly talking caught Mya's attention. Placing her feet with special care so as not to make any sound, she snuck forward toward the open door ahead to see what was prompting the argument, for argument it was, the whispering voices hissing at each other in obvious anger. As she drew nearer, Mya realized that one of the voices belonged to Kayden. He sounded angrier than the other, who was a woman.

There was the sound of a boot on a wood floor, and then as Mya dared to peek around the corner of the doorway, she saw that the sound had been one of them taking a step toward the other.

And they were kissing.

Mya froze in place, her mind trying to sort the details of what lay in front of her. Kayden was standing in the room, apparently a library, if the decor was anything to go by, and pressed up against him as though she had some right was Miss Blanche Auteberry, one of her skinny hands curled around the back of his neck. The realization had taken only the barest fraction of an instant. Kayden's right hand, Mya saw with a twist in her stomach, was on the other woman's hip, his left curled around her upper arm.

She might have just turned and left, left Kayden to Miss Auteberry and her bony, clutching hands, but that was the moment that the tart fell from fingers gone suddenly weak. It hit the ground loudly. Both Kayden and Miss Auteberry whipped around to see what the source of the sound was.

Miss Auteberry nearly stumbled back with how quickly she had broken apart from Kayden.

"Mya," Kayden said. "Fuck. Mya. This isn't—"

"No." Mya shook her head. "Absolutely not, Kayden McGregor. I don't care what your excuse is." She blinked back the burn of tears, refusing to let them fall in front of him. "Am I not good enough for you? Is that it? Maybe I'm not rich enough. Or maybe I don't talk the way I'm supposed to? Is that why?"

"No, Mya. None of that is—"

Kayden took a step forward as he spoke, but Blanche Auteberry stopped him, wrapping a hand around his arm and digging her nails in.

Mya turned and walked away, stepping deliberately in the chocolate tart on her way out. It seemed the chocolate would be wasted after all.

She had nearly reached the door when the sound of shoes following made her turn to see who was there. Blanche Auteberry was behind her, looking down her long nose at Mya as though she were regarding something she had scraped off her shoe. Ruined chocolate tart, for instance.

"What do you want?" Mya demanded.

"All of those suggestions you made back there as to why you are not enough? They are completely true," she said. "You have no income in your own right, and no inheritance. Your speech marks you very obviously as a member of the lower class, whatever claims you may make to the contrary, and the fact that Miss Alan and Miss MacLaren are wealthy and have chosen to take you in does not mean that you are qualified. Both of them are rich enough to have their eccentricities, but you do not have enough status to protect yourself from the rumors that go with them, nor from the rumors that go with you." She sniffed. "You need to move along now, Miss Boyle. This is not the place for one of your kind."

Mya suddenly wished, very fervently, that she hadn't wasted her chocolate tart by simply stepping on it. She would have dearly liked to throw it in Blanche Auteberry's face and watch it drip down her perfect white blouse.

"You've no need to worry about me," she said, tipping her chin up high. "I'm leaving. If you wish to keep Kayden, go right ahead. He's yours. Slightly used, or broken in. Whichever you prefer."

With that, she spun on her heel and stalked out the door, hurrying across the lawn and down into the garden that opened on the back fields. Kayden hadn't even come after her. Alone, she finally let the tears that had been threatening since the moment she saw them together fall.

How could he? After everything? Was it some sort of game to him? To see what he could get away with? He had already convinced her to take him back once. Maybe he wanted to know if he could do it a second time. But he would find that she wasn't so easy to convince.

The walk home was faster than the walk to Kayden's, driven by anger. When Mya swept up the garden path to the veranda, Lottie was still sitting on the bench, but she looked up at the sound of Mya's steps and, at the sight of her face, tossed the book aside without bothering to mark her place.

"Mya?" She crossed the porch and laid a hand on Mya's shoulder. "What is it?"

"You will never believe," Mya said, panting to catch her breath and stop the tears. "What I just saw."

Lottie tugged her gently toward the door and inside, guiding her to sit down at the dining table while she fetched her some water. She whispered something Mya couldn't hear to one of the maids, who rushed off.

"What happened?" Lottie asked, sinking into a chair and setting the water down in front of Mya.

"I went to Kayden's, as you know, to bring him some chocolate tart since the last one was somewhat ruined." She didn't even care anymore what Lottie thought of that. "When I arrived, there was a coach there. I thought perhaps he had a visitor, something work related, and I ought to have waited to see him until I had announced my intention to do so, but since I was already there, I went to deliver the tart."

The maid returned, just then, with a little plate of fruit and cheese, and Eleanora on her heels.

"And would you believe it," Mya said, choking back a sob. "His visitor was Miss Auteberry."

Lottie and Eleanora exchanged looks. She was sure they both knew where the story was going. It was rather obvious. She took a sip of the water Lottie had handed her to soothe the ache in her throat.

"They were kissing, when I saw them. When I left, he didn't even follow me. And then she came out and told me that I'm not rich and the two of you letting me stay here doesn't change that. And that my accent marks me as lower class, or some such nonsense." Mya's jaw tightened. "She told me that I'm not good enough for Kayden, and that his home wasn't the place for people of my kind. Whatever that means."

The words dissolved into tears, and Mya couldn't go on with the story. There wasn't much else to tell anyway. What had happened with the tart wasn't important.

"Oh, Mya." Lottie was there, then, a pair of warm arms wrapped around her, and Mya leaned into the other woman's chest, trying not to cry too much on her dress.

"She had no right," Eleanora said, voice tight.

"Of course she did not," Lottie said, stroking Mya's hair while Mya gave up on not ruining her clothing and just cried. "Though I daresay no one has ever taught her that there is a single thing in this world to which she is not entitled."

"How dare she speak that way to Mya." The anger that Mya had seen in Eleanora only once before was making its return. "If it would not be more trouble than it was worth, I would trip her into the loch and hope the monster eats her."

There was a moment of silence, and Mya looked up to find Lottie with a thoughtful expression on her face.

"You would have to drive her to the loch," she said after a moment. "And as I doubt Miss Auteberry would ever willingly step into a coach with either of us, I think that is rather unlikely. Not to mention the issue of an investigation." A smile slipped into the words. "If you are going to trip her, I suggest you do it somewhere you can deny having done it purposefully. Perhaps after a heavy rain."

"I did sincerely consider throwing the chocolate tart at her," Mya said. "But I had dropped it earlier and then stepped in it. I wish I had kept it."

Lottie's hand went back to stroking through Mya's hair, dislodging the pins she had so carefully put in it. "We will find a means of handling her," she said.

"I don't see how Kayden could have an explanation," Mya said then. "I saw them there. I saw them kiss. There's nothing he can say to me that is going to make me believe that he didn't do it."

"Believe me, Mya, we are not advising you to allow him back into your life," Eleanora said. "We would not do that to you."

"All the same, I would like to speak with him myself." Lottie sighed. "I just cannot imagine why he would do such a thing to Mya."

"If you want to talk to him," Mya said, "that's your choice. I won't stop you. But don't bring him here. I don't want to see his face."

"And if he does have an explanation?"

"If he does have an explanation," Mya laughed, "I will be utterly shocked. And unless an angel comes to tell me that Kayden was unfairly framed for the actions I saw unfolding directly in front of me, I am not taking him back."

After what he had done, she didn't want anything to do with Kayden McGregor ever again.

Chapter 18

"It would seem the Auteberrys are throwing another party," Lottie said one morning over breakfast, looking down at a piece of paper she was holding in her hand.

"I will not be attending," Mya said. It had been a week since the incident and the pain was still ripe like a fresh wound.

"Nor, I think, will I." Eleanora set an egg into the egg cup beside her plate and cracked the shell with a flick of her spoon. "Tell them that we have a previous engagement. Surely they cannot imagine that we would actually wish to be there, after what was done to Mya?"

"I am sure that Blanche has some sort of hand in this." Lottie's lips pressed flat together, her expression a study in disapproval. "It is likely she has orchestrated the whole thing in an attempt to upset Mya."

"I don't know why she'd need to," Mya said, picking at her toast without actually eating any of it. "She already has Kayden."

"I am not so certain about that," Lottie said.

Mya turned to look at her, not sure what the comment was supposed to mean. Lottie lifted her gaze from the bowl of yogurt in front of her to meet Mya's.

"I have not heard anything of them being seen together. In fact, Kayden has hardly been seen at all since the day you saw them together."

He had tried to come by the house, but this time there had been no letting him in, and if there were flowers Mya hadn't been told. She didn't care if he brought an entire greenhouse worth; she wasn't going to forgive him. He didn't deserve it.

"So Kayden is moping," Mya said, stabbing a sausage with her fork. "I don't see what that changes."

"There is no word that Kayden and Miss Auteberry are any sort of item," Lottie said. "I find that rather interesting, considering that she was supposed to be the more socially acceptable choice. Why would he not flaunt her? It is not as though he took you out. He would not have to explain why he had one girl on his arm one day and the next appeared with another."

That was true. The only time she had gone anywhere with Kayden that was not one of the back fields was when they had gone to the theater, and that hadn't been a social outing of the sort that he would take a woman he actually wished to be seen with. It had been one of the smaller playhouses, dark, and not the sort of place that attracted those accustomed to the social circles Mya had been traveling in since she came to live with Lottie and Ella.

"So he didn't take me out, and he doesn't take her out. Maybe he's just a terrible suitor," Mya suggested. "Although if that's the case, I don't know what he sees in Blanche. She will not be providing anything that he was getting from me, I'm quite sure."

Eleanora laughed.

"So if that is the case," Lottie said, "why has he not made his move with her? Because the only advantage he receives from a marriage with Miss Auteberry is her family's social clout to improve his own standing. Even that is somewhat dubious. He has a title of his own, and enough land and wealth that he will never need to worry about money. So what is the allure?"

"Maybe he just likes her," Mya said glumly. "That is something that happens sometimes between people, I've been told."

"If he was with her just because he chose to be, would he not be taking her out in public to show her off?" Eleanora asked.

"That is what I would expect, unless there was some secret they were keeping."

"Maybe he did receive something from her." Lottie took a sip of tea. "Or gave something to her, if you take my meaning."

"You think she's pregnant and that's why they're not going out in public?" Mya didn't even want to think about that. She stabbed the sausage again, ripping off a piece and taking a bite that didn't taste like anything except frustrated disappointment. "I don't think she is. And I don't understand it. He wanted me. I know he did. And we—"

She cut herself off. They had been over and over his interactions with her and how they meant he felt. Mya wasn't in the mood to rehash them.

"Anyway. I do not honestly see why we're having this discussion. None of it matters. We're not going to a party hosted by the Auteberrys, and Kayden can do whatever he pleases so long as it doesn't involve me."

"I suppose I just have a difficult time letting things go," Lottie said, lifting one shoulder and letting it fall again in a shrug. "I like to know what is going on, and why people do what they do."

"So go ask Kayden why he's an arse. I don't care, though. And I don't want to hear about what he has to say." Mya stood, leaving her hardly touched plate behind, and went back to her room. Behind her, as she left, she could hear a discussion starting that undoubtedly had something to do with her and Kayden. Let them talk about it. None of it mattered to her. She had other things to do.

It was raining the day after they received the invitation to the Auteberrys' ball. Mya looked out at the gray drizzle and sighed. It perfectly matched her mood, but the rain wouldn't be much of a boon for waking. She had hoped to get out of the house, and away from the looks that Lottie and Ella were still occasionally exchanging over her head, like they were worried about her but weren't quite sure how to approach the issue.

In the end, Mya decided a little rain had never done much harm, and dressed up in some of her warmer things to go walk in it anyway. At least it would give her something to do

The coat she wore kept the worst of the water off her, and Mya found she actually enjoyed wandering through the field all full of fog and water falling from the sky. There was a deeper scent to the heather, and the cool breeze was refreshing. Somewhere, there were frogs croaking softly, and Mya thought of the pond where she and Kayden had gone that day they rode up into the hills.

He had been so attentive to her there. Had looked at her as though she was the most beautiful thing he had ever seen, touched her as though she were something precious. How could he go from that to what he had done when she had walked in on him and Miss Auteberry? Had it all been an act, or had something somehow changed between them that she wasn't aware of?

Mya sighed, and dipped her head a little lower as the rain fell heavier, watching the toes of her boots move through the wet grass. She was glad she had worn the high ones, though the hem of her skirt was going to be soaked. She gathered up a little of it in each hand and tried to keep it from the worst of the mud.

"Mya?"

She stopped in her tracks. Kayden was not supposed to be there. It was not his land, and Lottie and Ella had told him in no uncertain terms that he was to keep off theirs. Mya had seen with her own eyes the message that they sent.

"Go away," she said, keeping her eyes on the ground. She started walking again.

"Mya, please. I just want to talk to you."

"And yet, I have no wish to speak to you. Go home, Kayden."

"I didn't kiss her!"

Slowly, Mya turned around to face him. "What was that?"

Kayden, who was standing in front of her not wearing any sort of protection from the rain at all, leaned closer, his eyes pleading. "I didn't kiss Miss Auteberry, Mya. I know what you think you saw, but she kissed me, not the other way around. And I pushed her off."

Mya laughed bitterly. "Do you really think I am going to fall for that lie? It is as old as time. And I was standing right there. You didn't push her off. And you didn't even speak to me. If you didn't kiss her, why didn't you come after me when I walked away?"

"My hand was on her arm to shove her away. She was clinging to me like a limpet!"

"Why don't you tell this story to someone who cares?" Mya asked, turning away to continue on her walk.

Kayden's hand on her arm stopped her. It was gentle, not the clutching desperation visible in Blanche's touch when she had grabbed Kayden after the kiss.

"I swear, Mya. I didn't kiss her. I didn't want to. You are the only woman that I want. Ever. Always."

She wrenched her arm out of his hold. "Then why didn't you come after me when I left? You just let her follow and berate me, tell me how poor and worthless I was and how I was no good for you? If you really cared, you would've stopped her. If you truly cared, Kayden, you would have tried to stop *me*. But you didn't."

"I did try to come after you," Kayden said. "Her maid came up out of nowhere and grabbed me, babbling about some kind of emergency with the stable and one of my servants. By the time I had been dragged out to see that nothing was actually wrong, you were back home, and Lottie wouldn't let me in."

"Lottie wouldn't let you in because I asked her not to. Because you're an ass, and I didn't want to see you."

But the words didn't hold the venom of her earlier accusations. Had Kayden truly tried to come after her? If he had, if he was telling the truth, that meant Blanche and her maid must have somehow planned the whole thing. Had one of them seen her coming up the walk? She supposed there were enough rumors about her and Kayden by now that someone must have figured out what was going on, and it had gone back to Blanche.

"How can I be sure you're telling the truth?"

Kayden took a step forward, obviously encouraged by the fact that she was even willing to consider listening to him. As she watched, he went to one knee in the wet grass, likely completely ruining his suit. His hair was plastered to his head, dripping down into his eyes. He reached out, slowly enough that she could have pulled away if she had wanted to.

"Mya," he said when her hands were held in his. "You are everything that I desire."

Her mouth twisted. "Truly? This sort of flowery garbage, Kayden? I thought you were better than this."

"Would you just listen to me? I am trying to say something to you here, Mya."

Despite herself, Mya felt one corner of her mouth trying to twitch upward into a smile at the look on his face. She waved a silent "go on" in his direction.

"I am going to say something," he repeated. "And I don't care how ridiculous or flowery it is. Nothing in this world has ever made me as happy as you do, Mya. And I do not care if I have to wait a year. Or ten years. Or twenty. I do not care if it takes a hundred. I will wait until you are ready to have me again, because I would rather have you laughing at me than another woman fawning for my approval. You have won me utterly, and there is no time or place in which I am not ardently and desperately yours." His eyes locked with her own. "I would give you the universe entire were it mine to give, but if you will settle for just myself, I will be the most blessed man in all of history."

Mya stared down at him. He was still kneeling there, looking utterly pathetic in the rain. She thought of the nights they had spent together, and the way that his hands felt on her skin. The way that he had always treated her as though she mattered. The laughter they had shared.

"You swear to me that you do not want Blanche?" Her voice trembled a little on the words.

"I swear it," Kayden said. "On everything that has ever been dear to me."

Giddy laughter bubbled up in Mya's chest and overflowed. Laughing, she lifted Kayden to his feet, and then he was there, crowding into her space and claiming her mouth with his own. Kissing her until neither of them were breathing anything but the other.

Chapter 19

After much consideration, Mya decided to go to the Auteberrys' ball. Not to confront Blanche, she argued with herself, but to simply show that she was above what the woman had said and done. When she explained the situation to Lottie and Eleanora, both had stared at her like she was crazy. It likely didn't help that she made the announcement just after meeting Kayden in the rain, as they both stood, dripping all over the rug.

"You are certain about this?" Lottie asked, her eyes moving from Mya to Kayden and back and forth between them.

"Very. Kayden's sure. We're both sure."

Lottie's and Ella's heads moved at the same time to stare at Kayden, who nodded. The way he looked at Mya must have confirmed everything. Or maybe the way he couldn't stop staring at her.

"In that case," Lottie said, clapping her hands together with a grin that Mya thought looked a little too dangerous. "We're going to want new dresses. All of us." She winked at Kayden. "Except you. Maybe a new suit?"

From that moment on, everything became about getting ready for the party. As it had been the first time, there were dress fittings and new gloves, new hats and shoes. But this time, there was also Kayden.

He didn't take Mya out, but that was her choice as much as his. Neither of them had wanted Blanche or anyone connected to the Auteberrys to see them together. It would ruin the revelation. It needed to be an eye-opener for Blanche. And Mya was very much looking forward to that bit of theater. She was quite sure Blanche would never forget it.

The day of the ball dawned cloudy and gray, but Mya refused to let it dampen her spirits.

"I hope you are aware," Eleanora said as they readied themselves to leave that afternoon, "that what you are doing will be quite a shock to the community. They will not stop speaking of it for some time, and there will be varying opinions on the matter. Most of them negative. People will treat you with concealed if not outright disdain."

"I don't care," Mya answered. "If everyone in the world is against me, as long as I have Kayden, I will be fine. He makes me strong."

Eleanora reached out and laid a hand over her wrist, stopping Mya from reaching for the bracelet she had been about to put on and waiting until Mya turned and met her eyes before speaking. "It will not be everyone in the world, of that I can assure you. You will always have my support, and Lottie's."

On impulse, Mya took a step forward and wrapped her arms around the other woman, pulling her into a tight hug. For a moment, Eleanora was startled stiff in the embrace, and then she softened and returned it. When she moved back a moment later, she was smiling.

"Your decision," she said, "might be an outrageous one, but it is the right one. People forget, in all this pageantry, what true emotion is. Love, when it is true, is worth more than all the social status or money in the world."

Lottie rushed in just then, looking for the necklace she had meant to wear to the dance, which she could not find, and the moment was broken. Eleanora, laying a calming hand on her shoulder, went to help her retrieve it. As the sound of their footsteps retreated, Mya turned to the mirror and stood looking in it, studying the face that looked back at her. She did not look like someone about to make an outrageous decision, she thought. Nor did she feel like it. She felt... calm. As though there was no other decision that could have been made.

She supposed there was, of course. They could have gone a more socially approved route. But Kayden was determined that everyone know he wanted to be with her, it was his way of declaring publicly that he did not care about her lack of family or her financial state, did not care about the political connections that he could make by marrying Blanche. And if he wished the world to know where he stood on those matters, Mya was more than happy to help him demonstrate.

The carriage ride over was an exercise in patience. Mya watched the landscape slide by outside the window, tapping a finger against her knee. She was ready to be there. Ready for it all to be over and Kayden to be officially hers.

"You are sure you want to do this?" Lottie asked, watching her.

Mya looked up. "Yes. I am sure. Do I look like I am not?"

"You look nervous."

"No." Mya shook her head, smiling slightly. "Not nervous. Impatient."

Lottie laughed. "In that case, then, dear, you will have your moment soon enough. Wait, and enjoy it for what it is."

It was good advice. Mya sighed, and tried to follow it. Still, she was grateful when they arrived at the Auteberrys' estate. They stepped down from the carriage and went inside, once more introduced by the butler. She saw several heads turn, and wondered if any of them were close friends of Blanche, if they were expecting an entirely different end to the night than the one she and Kayden had planned. If they were mocking her behind their polite smiles.

Lottie's gown was a blue so deep it was nearly purple, and this time it was she who wore bluebells in her hair. Eleanora, in pale green touched with silver, had sprays of heather in her chignon, and Mya smiled to see so many eyes follow her and Lottie through the room. Mya's own gown was layer upon layer of sky blue lace, its edges fluttering gently with her motion. She felt rather like she thought royalty might, making her way over to the side to be seated and feeling all eyes on her.

Kayden had not seen the dress yet; she had wished it to be a surprise. But she was rather certain he was going to like it.

The night went on, at first, as it had the last time they had attended such a ball. Mya's dance card filled up, though she was careful to set aside several for Kayden, and she saw Lottie and Eleanora on the arms of various partners, both of them looking as though they were enjoying the night.

When Kayden arrived, the dance had been in full swing for nearly an hour. The butler called his name, and then he was moving down the stairs and into the ballroom. The Auteberrys moved to intercept him.

Mya wondered what Blanche Auteberry had told her parents. They were undoubtedly involved in the attempt to marry her to Kayden. She watched them smile and nod and present Blanche in her lilac-colored gown to Kayden, whose face was impassive. A moment later, he glanced up and his eyes met Mya's through the bustle of the crowd. She smiled at him.

He let Blanche take his arm, and lead him out onto the dance floor. She clung to him in a way that almost verged on impropriety, and Mya resisted the urge to stalk out into the middle of the dance and pull her from his arms.

As the dance continued, she watched from the sidelines, saw Kayden lean down to say something to Blanche, likely whispered in her ear to be heard over the music.

Blanche's expression went from pleased to startled. And then from startled to angry. She moved to step back, but Kayden held her for a moment longer, bent his head to her ear to say one last thing. When she jerked herself from his arms, the dancers around her faltered.

She knocked into the couple that had been behind her, and turned immediately to apologize. The dance had lost its orderly motion, and the rhythms were crumbling. The music fumbled and stopped. In the sudden silence, Mya could hear her heart beating loudly in her ears.

Blanche, obviously realizing that she had every eye in the place on her, spun on her heel and stalked away without saying a word. Mya's heart beat faster. This was the moment that they had planned for. Kayden was making his way through the crowd. Lottie and Eleanora, Mya suddenly noticed, had reappeared, and were standing just to the side, watching her. Close enough that they could step in if something went wrong, she suspected.

And then Kayden was there. And he was going to one knee in front of her. A murmur ran through the crowd, but Mya hardly heard it. She had expected him to show that he was courting her, not thing. But looking down into Kayden's dark eyes, her entire world consumed by the want and warmth and love laid bare there. Everyone in the room disappeared, except for him.

"Mya Boyle," he said. "In the time that I have known you, you have altered my world utterly. I cannot imagine it now without you in it, cannot imagine a life without you by my side. I am completely and devotedly in love with you, and nothing in this world would make me happier than for you to be my wife. Will you consent to marry me?"

She hadn't known the proposal was coming. Without needing to consider the question, she knew what her answer was. She couldn't stop the joy from rushing up through her like a tide, filling her chest and making her throat tight and her eyes prickle with happy tears.

"Yes," she said, realizing only as it left her that the word was a whisper hardly loud enough to be heard. "Yes," she said again, louder and laughing with pleasure. "I will marry you, Kayden McGregor."

He was on his feet in the next moment, sliding a silver ring with a lover's knot in the band onto her finger and taking her hands in both of his. There was a wide smile on his face. Mya was laughing. Distantly, from the corner of her eye, she noted Blanche and her parents watching from the other side of the ballroom, their expressions horrified. Mya didn't care. She had everything she needed right in front of her.

They were thrown out of the ball. Mya had half expected it. Kayden had gone against their hosts when he'd chosen her over Blanche; it was hardly a surprise that they wished to see neither him nor Mya in their house. Lottie and Eleanor, though they likely would have been grudgingly allowed to remain, had come with them.

"You have succeeded," Eleanora said, "in becoming the most talked about couple in Inverness tonight."

Mya laughed. "Yes. I imagine that we have."

Kayden handed her up into his coach, and Mya slid onto the seat, straightening out her skirts. A moment later, he followed her up. The door closed behind him, and then he was pulling her into his arms. Kissing her hard. Mya wrapped her arms around his neck and kissed him in return.

When they broke apart, Kayden was smiling again.

Mya felt an answering grin on her own face. "That went better than I expected," she admitted.

He laughed, gathering her up and pulling her into his lap, his arm supporting her shoulders. "Did you expect it to go badly, then?"

Mya shook her head, not sure how to put into words the feeling she'd had. "I just... I thought there might be a catch or something. It was such an astonishing thing to the people in there, but I suppose they'll content themselves with gossip and refusing to speak to us later."

Kayden's fingers curled gently under her chin, lifting her head to meet her eyes. "No catch," he said gently. "We were meant to be together. No moment in time can tear us apart."

"I love you, Kayden McGregor," Mya said, voice catching a little over the words.

"And I love you," he answered. "Utterly."

"And forever," Mya said.

"And forever."

Epilogue

Eleanora had been right about the way people would react. In the week since Mya had accepted Kayden's proposal, most people would not look at her on the street in Inverness. There were no invitations to parties or socials. Occasionally she thought she caught a friendly look, but she could never be quite sure. Mya didn't care. The rest of the world could do as it pleased. She had Kayden, and that was all that mattered.

The ride that day was Kayden's idea.

They packed a picnic as they had before, riding up into the hills. This time, though, they were not alone. Lottie and Eleanora rode with them, and they talked as they rode, chatting and laughing. Mya grinned up at the blue sky overhead and wondered if it was possible to be any happier than she was in that moment. The man she loved most in the world rode at her side, his ring on her finger, and her best friends were close by. They had already started talking wedding plans, Lottie insisting on having it at their manor, a plan to which Kayden had readily acquiesced, so long as there was chocolate tart.

"I have been considering the flowers we might use," Lottie said as they came over a rise toward the pond where Kayden and Mya had picnicked before.

Mya laughed. "There are topics of conversation other than my wedding, you know."

"Is that a subtle hint that you would prefer to discuss things other than your wedding?" Lottie asked, grinning at her.

"I believe it is," Eleanora said on her other side.

"You treat me so unkindly," Lottie gasped, laying a dramatic hand to her forehead. "I do not know how I survive it with such grace."

Mya and Eleanora exchanged glances, and burst into laughter. Kayden's deep rumble joined them. Lottie threw her hands in the air and gave her horse a nudge forward, kicking him into a canter. Her happy shout echoed back to them as she raced ahead. Mya looked back at Kayden, who shook his head, smiling.

"Go on, then."

With a laugh, Mya sent her mount racing after Lottie's, watching the scenery blur. Ahead, Lottie was slowing a little, and Mya leaned closer over her horse's neck. She was going to catch up.

In the next instant, something white darted out in front of the horse.

The mare reared, whinnying alarm. Mya tried to hold to her, but the grip was wrong. She struggled a moment, as if in slow motion, and then fell.

Pain lanced through her. She thought she heard Kayden cry out behind her, Eleanora's voice rising above his. When she opened her eyes, she saw the white stag, standing at the edge of the tree line and looking back at her. Lottie was shouting.

I'm fine, she meant to say. *I am fine.*

But the words couldn't seem to line up as they should.

Kayden reached her first. She heard the horse come to an abrupt stop, and then he was leaning over her, one hand on her forehead and the other reaching for hers.

Mya closed her fingers around his; dots and lights seemed to be dancing in her eyes.

"Mya," he said, speaking too quickly. "Mya. Darling. Look at me. You are going to be fine. Just look at me. Don't close your eyes."

She tried to obey him, despite the ache in her head and the heaviness of her eyelids, looking up to meet his gaze. Dimly, she could hear Lottie and Eleanora in the background, and then the sound of hooves racing away. Someone going for the doctor.

"Stay, Mya. You were made to be with me, as I was made to love you. No moment in time can take that away from us. Stay with me, Mya, please."

"Kayden..." Even that single word was hard to say.

Looking up at him, she felt as though this had happened before. Her in his arms, his tearful gaze pleading with her to stay. She felt as though...

A little house, full of firelight. The garden. Kayden, standing behind her with his arms guiding hers as she pulled back the string of a bow.

"I remember you," she said.

"What? Mya?"

She reached up, pressing her palm to his cheek. "I remember you," she said again. "My Highlander."

His eyes widened. She could almost see the memories running through them, flickering behind them like firelight. He shook his head.

"No," he said sharply. "No, Mya. Not again. Don't you do this to me again. Not like this."

He was leaning down over her, holding her hand almost painfully tight. Tears streaked down his face.

"Don't leave me, Mya. Not again. Don't leave me."

"I love you, Kayden McGregor," Mya whispered. "Forever."

She gave in to the pull of the darkness, and closed her eyes.

THE END
Modern Day Bride

Modern Day Bride: Moment in Time #3

You were made to be with me, as I was made to love you. No moment in time can take that away from us.

The sounds of a storm wakes Mya in the middle of the night. Except instead of a storm, a war is raging outside the window. She had no idea what time it is, or even the date. She doesn't know how she ended up in the building, or who the handsome soldier that saves her is.

She feels connected to him, and his older worldly ways. A stranger and yet she knows things about him—intimate things, like the scar on his chest, the way his hair curls around her fingers when she runs her hand through it.

Pieces of a puzzle they don't understand, begin to fit together. Destiny seems to be pushing them together, but why? Just when they are on the verge of figuring out their connection, the devastating war tears them apart again.

You were given this life because you're strong enough to live it.

A Moment in Time Series

Highlander's Bride
Book 1
Victorian Bride
Book 2
Modern Day Bride
Book 3
A Royal Bride
Book 4
Forever the Bride
Book 5

More by Lexy Timms:

Book One is FREE!

Sometimes the heart needs a different kind of saving... find out if Charity Thompson will find a way of saving forever in this hospital setting Best-Selling Romance by Lexy Timms

Charity Thompson wants to save the world, one hospital at a time. Instead of finishing med school to become a doctor, she chooses a different path and raises money for hospitals – new wings, equipment, whatever they need. Except there is one hospital she would be happy to never set foot in again—her fathers. So of course he hires her to create a gala for his sixty-fifth birthday. Charity can't say no. Now she is working in the one place she doesn't want to be. Except she's attracted to Dr. Elijah Bennet, the handsome playboy chief.

Will she ever prove to her father that's she's more than a med school dropout? Or will her attraction to Elijah keep her from repairing the one thing she desperately wants to fix?

** This is NOT Erotica. It's Romance and a love story. **

* This is Part 1 of an Eight book Romance Series. It does end on a cliff-hanger*

Managing the Bosses Series
The Boss
Book 1 IS FREE!

Jamie Connors has given up on finding a man. Despite being smart, pretty, and just slightly overweight, she's a magnet for the kind of guys that don't stay around.

Her sister's wedding is at the foreground of the family's attention. Jamie would be find with it if her sister wasn't pressuring her to lose weight so she'll fit in the maid of honor dress, her mother would get off her case and her ex-boyfriend wasn't about to become her brother-in-law.

Determined to step out on her own, she accepts a PA position from billionaire Alex Reid. The job includes an apartment on his property and gets her out of living in her parent's basement.

Jamie has to balance her life and somehow figure out how to manage her billionaire boss, without falling in love with him.

Hades' Spawn MC Series
One You Can't Forget
Book 1 is FREE

Emily Rose Dougherty is a good Catholic girl from mythical Walkerville, CT. She had somehow managed to get herself into a heap trouble with the law, all because an ex-boyfriend has decided to make things difficult.

Luke "Spade" Wade owns a Motorcycle repair shop and is the Road Captian for Hades' Spawn MC. He's shocked when he reads in the paper that his old high school flame has been arrested. She's always been the one he couldn't forget.

Will destiny let them find each other again? Or what happens in the past, best left for the history books?

The Recruiting Trip

Aspiring college athlete Aileen Nessa is finding the recruiting process beyond daunting. Being ranked #10 in the world for the 100m hurdles at the age of eighteen is not a fluke, even though she believes that one race, where everything clinked magically together, might be. American universities don't seem to think so. Letters are pouring in from all over the country.

As she faces the challenge of differentiating between a college's genuine commitment to her or just empty promises from talent-seeking coaches, Aileen heads to the University of Gatica, a Division One school, on a recruiting trip. Her best friend dares who to go just to see the cute guys on the school's brochure.

The university's athletic program boasts one of the top hurdlers in the country. Tyler Jensen is the school's NCAA champion in the hurdles and Jim Thorpe recipient for top defensive back in football. His incredible blue-green eyes, confident smile and rock hard six pack abs mess with Aileen's concentration.

His offer to take her under his wing, should she choose to come to Gatica, is a temping proposition that has her wondering if she might be with an angel or making a deal with the devil himself.

Seeking Justice
Book 1 – is FREE

Rachel Evans has the life most people could only dream of: the promise of an amazing job, good looks, and a life of luxury. The problem is, she hates it. She tries desperately to avoid getting sucked into the family business and hides her wealth and name from her friends. She's seen her brother trapped in that life, and doesn't want it. When her father dies in a plane crash, she reluctantly steps in to become the vice president of her family's company, Syco Pharmaceuticals.

Detective Adrien Deluca and his partner have been called in to look at the crash. While Adrien immediately suspects not everything about the case is what it seems, he has trouble convincing his partner. However, soon into the investigation, they uncover a web of deceit which proves the crash was no accident, and evidence points toward a shadowy group of people. Now the detective needs find the proof.

To what lengths will Deluca go to get it?

Fortune Riders MC Series
NOW AVAILABLE!

Undercover Series - Book 1, PERFECT FOR ME, is FREE!

The city of Pittsburgh keeps its streets safe, partly thanks to Lt. Grady Rivers. The police officer is fiercely intelligent who specializes in undercover operations. It is this set of skills that are sought by New York's finest. Grady is thrown from his hometown onto the New York City underworld in order to stop one of the largest drug rings in the northeast. The NYPD task him with uncovering the identity of the organization's mysterious leader, Dean. It will take all of his cunning to stop this deadly drug lord.

Danger lurks around every corner and comes in many shapes. While undercover, he meets a beauty named Lara. An equally intelligent woman and twice as fearless, she works for a local drug dealer who has ties to the organization. Their sorted pasts have these two become close, and soon they develop feelings for one another. But this is not a "Romeo and Juliet" love story, as the star-crossed lovers fight to survive the deadly streets. Grady treads the thin line between the love he feels for her, and his duties as an officer.

Will he get in too deep?

Heart of the Battle Series
Celtic Viking
Book 1

In a world plagued with darkness, she would be his salvation.
No one gave Erik a choice as to whether he would fight or not. Duty to the crown belonged to him, his father's legacy remaining beyond the grave.
Taken by the beauty of the countryside surrounding her, Linzi would do anything to protect her father's land. Britain is under attack and Scotland is next. At a time she should be focused on suitors, the men of her country have gone to war and she's left to stand alone.
Love will become available, but will passion at the touch of the enemy unravel her strong hold first?
Fall in love with this Historical Celtic Viking Romance.
* There are 3 books in this series. Book 1 will end on a cliff hanger.
*Note: this is NOT erotica. It is a romance and a love story.

Knox Township, August 1863.

Little Love Affair, Book 1 in the Southern Romance series, by bestselling author Lexy Timms

Sentiments are running high following the battle of Gettysburg, and although the draft has not yet come to Knox, "Bloody Knox" will claim lives the next year as citizens attempt to avoid the Union draft. Clara's brother Solomon is missing, and Clara has been left to manage the family's farm, caring for her mother and her younger sister, Cecelia.

Meanwhile, wounded at the battle of Monterey Pass but still able to escape Union forces, Jasper and his friend Horace are lost and starving. Jasper wants to find his way back to the Confederacy, but feels honor-bound to bring Horace back to his family, though the man seems reluctant.

Now Available:

Coming Soon:

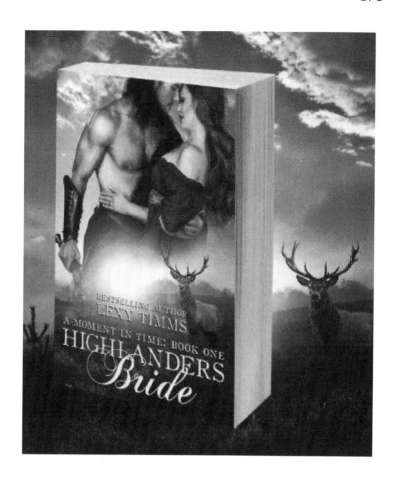

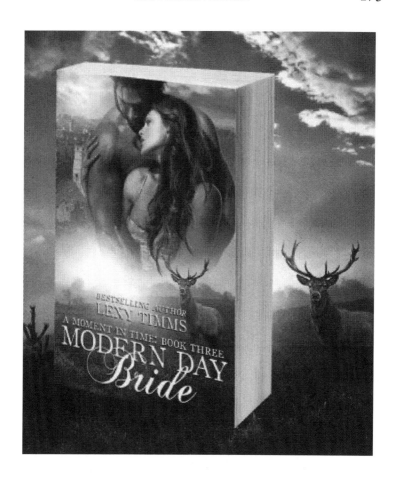

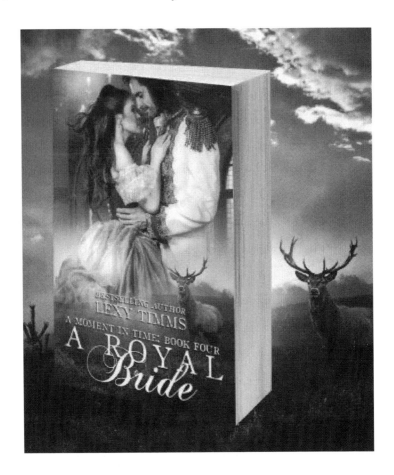

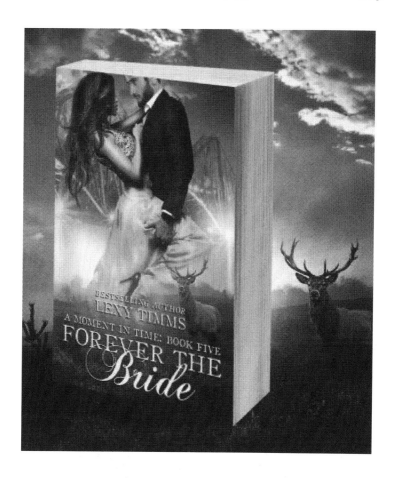

Don't miss out!

Click the button below and you can sign up to receive emails whenever Lexy Timms publishes a new book. There's no charge and no obligation.

Sign Me Up!

https://books2read.com/r/B-A-NNL-DTFL

Connecting independent readers to independent writers.

Did you love *Victorian Bride*? Then you should read *Unknown* by Lexy Timms!

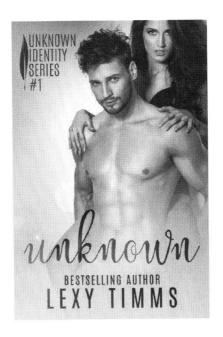

Bestselling romance author, Lexy Timms, brings you a new billionaire contemporary romance series that'll steal your heart and take your breath away.

Unknown - book 1 of the Unknown Identity Series

Life has changed radically for Leslie. Her husband has finally succumbed to his terminal cancer and it's time for her to have a change of scenery. Moving across the country and setting up shop, Leslie takes the months to rebuild her life and figure out what she wants in the future.

Pouring herself into her successful mystery books series she's written, she is a reclusive global sensation writing under a penname.

Leslie realizes that her life is missing the romance she so desperately craved and now she's on the hunt to live her life beyond her grief.

Sooner than she realizes, cupid comes calling in the form of a handsome actor who has no clue she's a successful author. However, he comes with his own personal set of baggage.

Is new love possible after you've laid true love to rest?

Unknown Identity Series

Book 1 - Unknown

Book 2 - Unpublished

Book 3 - Unexposed

Also by Lexy Timms

Alpha Bad Boy Motorcycle Club Triology
Alpha Biker

Conquering Warrior Series
Ruthless

Diamond in the Rough Anthology
Billionaire Rock
Billionaire Rock - part 2

Dominating PA Series
Her Personal Assistant - Part 1
Her Personal Assistant - Part 2
Her Personal Assistant - Part 3
Her Personal Assistant Box Set

Firehouse Romance Series
Caught in Flames
Burning With Desire
Craving the Heat
Firehouse Romance Complete Collection

Fortune Riders MC Series
Billionaire Biker
Billionaire Ransom
Billionaire Misery

Hades' Spawn Motorcycle Club
One You Can't Forget
One That Got Away

One That Came Back
One You Never Leave
Hades' Spawn MC Complete Series

Heart of the Battle Series
Celtic Viking
Celtic Rune
Celtic Mann
Heart of the Battle Series Box Set

Justice Series
Seeking Justice
Finding Justice
Chasing Justice
Pursuing Justice
Justice - Complete Series

Love You Series
Love Life: Billionaire Dance School Hot Romance
Need Love

Managing the Bosses Series
The Boss
The Boss Too
Who's the Boss Now
Love the Boss
I Do the Boss
Wife to the Boss
Employed by the Boss
Brother to the Boss
Senior Advisor to the Boss
Forever the Boss
Gift for the Boss - Novella 3.5

Moment in Time
Highlander's Bride
Victorian Bride
Modern Day Bride

R&S Rich and Single Series
Alex Reid
Parker

Saving Forever
Saving Forever - Part 1
Saving Forever - Part 2
Saving Forever - Part 3
Saving Forever - Part 4
Saving Forever - Part 5
Saving Forever - Part 6
Saving Forever Part 7
Saving Forever - Part 8

Southern Romance Series
Little Love Affair
Siege of the Heart
Freedom Forever
Soldier's Fortune

Tattooist Series
Confession of a Tattooist
Surrender of a Tattooist
Heart of a Tattooist

Tennessee Romance
Whisky Lullaby
Whisky Melody
Whisky Harmony

The Debt
The Debt: Part 1 - Damn Horse
The Debt: Complete Collection

The University of Gatica Series
The Recruiting Trip
Faster
Higher
Stronger
Dominate
No Rush

Undercover Series
Perfect For Me
Perfect For You
Perfect For Us

Unknown Identity Series
Unknown
Unexposed
Unpublished

Standalone
Wash
Loving Charity
Summer Lovin'
Christmas Magic: A Romance Anthology
Love & College
Billionaire Heart
First Love
Frisky and Fun Romance Box Collection
Managing the Bosses Box Set #1-3

Made in the USA
Lexington, KY
01 June 2017